Other Sharon McCone mysteries by Marcia Muller

Edwin of the Iron Shoes
Ask the Cards a Question
The Cheshire Cat's Eye
Games to Keep the Dark Away

LEAVE A MESSAGE FOR WILLIE

by Marcia Muller

St. Martin's Press
New York

Design by Kingsley Parker.

Library of Congress Cataloging in Publication Data
Muller, Marcia.
  Leave a message for Willie.
  I. Title.
PS3563.U397L4 1984   813' .54   84-13346
ISBN 0-312-47728-7

First Edition

10 9 8 7 6 5 4 3 2 1

For Mary DeYoe and Terry Milne

chapter one

"You want any of those paintbrushes, they're all half price."

The vendor, in cut-off jeans and a baseball cap, loomed over me as I squatted, considering his wares. I rocked back on my heels and looked up at him. "Business is slow, huh?"

"Nah, I'm generous, is all. Half price, and you buy ten brushes, I'll knock off another dollar."

"What on earth would I do with ten of them?"

He grinned, his suntanned face creasing into deep lines. "Open your own stall. That's how I got started in the flea market business."

"I'll take two." I stood up and fumbled in my bag for change.

The man shook his head. "Some people wouldn't know a bargain if it bit them on the ass."

I waggled the brushes at him and started down the crowded aisle, looking for my friend Don.

The Saltflats Flea Market was spread over several acres sandwiched between the Bayshore Freeway and the frontage road, near the little town of Brisbane. During the week, it was nothing but a barren, rock-strewn plain; but on Saturdays and Sundays, the vendors streamed in. They erected booths with colorful canopies or sold their goods from blankets on the ground. Balloons flew, banners waved, and music—from dozens of radios, most tuned to country-and-western stations—filled the air.

I weaved down the aisle, avoiding baby strollers and a kid on a bicycle, and spotted Don at a stand featuring stereo equipment. He was closing in on a bunch of speakers with an ardent disc-jockey gleam in his eye, and I quickened my pace, knowing I'd better get him out of there, fast. By the time I reached him, he was crawling on his hands and knees, examining the connections at the back of one speaker. I nudged his foot with mine and he looked up, his expression blank for a moment.

1

"It's me. Sharon. Remember?"

"Oh, yeah. We've met someplace. Give me a minute and I'll figure out where." Then he looked back at the speaker, a shade wistfully. "These are a terrific deal."

"Of course they are. They're probably hot."

Don straightened up to his full six foot two, brushing dirt off his hands. He raised one dark eyebrow and waited.

"A lot of the stuff they sell here is," I went on. "Some of the vendors are legitimate business people and craftsmen, but quite a bit of fencing goes on too."

Don continued to wait, stroking his shaggy black mustache, his hazel eyes interested. At the beginning of our relationship I'd taken this quiet interest to be boredom—mainly because he'd struck me as such a motormouth when we'd first met. But, as we'd become closer and more comfortable with one another, I'd realized he only chattered when he was nervous or felt he needed to be on stage. Don Del Boccio, star disc jockey of a mid-coastal radio station, conserved his words in his private life as much as he squandered them on the air.

"This particular flea market," I said, "has a reputation for tolerating illegal activity. I myself just bought what are probably hot paintbrushes to use on the trim in the living room."

Don put an arm around me and began steering me through the crowd. "You bought hot merchandise when you're here on a mission of law and order?"

"I wouldn't label meeting with a prospective client as 'a mission of law and order.' But I did promise my boss I'd look the guy up, so I guess I'd better quit wandering around and try to locate him; supposedly he has a stall here."

"Why not ask one of the other vendors? Maybe the guy at the snow-cone stand can tell you. I'll treat you to a cone."

"Okay. A rainbow one, please."

The snow-cone vendor was a tall black man in a satin shirt and silver-studded jeans. I wondered how he could stand the noontime heat in that getup, but he looked as cool as the ice he was shaping into cones. When Don asked for two, the man took them and deftly began adding syrup from the big plastic dispensers.

"First you put on some blue," he said in what was probably a standard spiel. "For the sky. Then add yellow. For sunshine. And now"—he flourished the cones dramatically—"red. For excitement!" With a bow he handed them to us. "There you are, folks."

The three kinds of syrup had begun to run together. I tasted mine and felt a sudden, sharp pang of nostalgia for my childhood. When I looked at Don, he had red ice stuck in his swooping mustache.

I laughed and said, "Hold this for a second, will you?" When he took the cone I reached into my bag and got out the card that my boss, Hank Zahn of All Souls Legal Cooperative, had given me the previous afternoon. Printed in black on gold metallic stock, it read:

NEED STUFF FOR FLEA MARKETS?
CALL 755-4200
LEAVE A MESSAGE FOR WILLIE

I handed the card to the snow-cone vendor. "Do you know where I can find Willie Whelan?"

"Everybody knows Willie." He gave the card back without looking at it. "Go to the end there, turn left, and take the third aisle. He'll be midway down on the right, set up in front of a brand-new red pickup truck."

"Thanks." I retrieved my snow cone from Don, and we started off in the direction the man had pointed.

The cone was melting fast, and I tilted the paper cup clumsily, smearing the sticky liquid on my face and hands. Don, used to my minor mishaps by now, merely rolled his eyes as I fished out a Kleenex. "Well, it's melting faster than it should," I said, scrubbing at my chin.

"I know." He squeezed my shoulder and continued eating his own cone, which seemed to be surviving just fine.

It *was* a hot day for May. We'd had an early spring and already the hills above Brisbane, a village only miles south of San Francisco, were turning brown. The wild grasses around the perimeter of the flea market were baked to a wheat color and the bay, beyond the cars that whizzed by on the freeway, looked like a desert mirage. I pulled my cotton blouse free from my damp back, wishing I'd worn something cooler.

"Hey, babe," Don said, "there's something that's absolutely you."

I looked where he pointed. It was a pair of roller skates with bright green vinyl shoes. They stood among an assortment of rumpled used clothing, some in cardboard boxes, some merely

3

heaped on the ground. I started to laugh, then looked guiltily around for the seller. He was curled up on the ground under a scabrous old van, as limp as the clothing and totally oblivious to us.

We continued along past stands offering assorted junk, houseplants, hand-thrown pottery, dried fruit, nuts, olives, and honey. There were fake oriental rugs, real live rabbits, books, posters, and bright red popcorn. A sign on a box of records read THESE ALBUMS 25¢. (NOT ALL ARE SHITTY.) One stall advertised a "crazy sale"—any post-season quilted Easter basket, complete with green celluloid grass, for a dollar. Behind a glass case full of hunting knives, a smiling fat man sat under a miniature beach umbrella that attached to his head like a halo in a child's Christmas play. I glanced at his sinister-looking wares, grimaced, and moved on.

A beat-up Chevy piled high with junk edged along the crowded aisle, beeping its horn, and some of the kids jumped on its bumper. The driver began to inch into an empty space to the accompaniment of good-natured jeers and catcalls. As we waited for the car to move out of our way, I spied the red pickup truck pulled up in a large space on the right. There were no vehicles within ten or twelve feet on either side of it, as if its shiny newness deserved more room than others. Pointing to it, I grabbed Don's hand and we squeezed around the slow-moving Chevy.

Willie Whelan's concession was of the assorted-junk variety— but a much higher quality of junk than we'd seen up to now. Several shabby Oriental rugs were spread on the ground in front of the truck, and on them was arranged a truly fascinating accumulation of objects. There were three old pedestal-type sinks and a clawfooted bathtub; four or five newel posts that had been converted to plant stands; illuminated beer signs, Depression glassware, and a whole stack of drip coffeemakers still in the manufacturer's packaging; old mantel clocks, new clock radios, and a cello. Near the truck stood a player piano. At the very front was a huge birdcage, complete with parrot.

I glanced from the beady-eyed bird to the truck and spotted a man sitting on its tailgate. He was in his late thirties, wearing Levi's, a leather vest, and a cowboy hat. When he saw Don and me, he unfolded his tall, lanky frame and ambled over. His cleanshaven face was open and amiable, his eyes, above a slightly hooked nose, a startling shade of blue.

"Help you folks?" It was the same voice I'd heard on the phone the night before.

"You're Willie Whelan?"

"That's the name." He held out a hand and I grasped it briefly.

"I'm Sharon McCone. And this—" I turned to introduce Don, but he had gone over to inspect the claw-footed bathtub, probably with the idea it might do for my new house. "That," I said, "is my friend Don Del Boccio."

Willie took off his cowboy hat and smoothed down his curly brown hair before carefully resettling the hat. "He a detective too?"

"No, a houseguest."

He nodded. "Well, he looks like he can amuse himself. Why don't you come back to the truck? We'll talk, have a beer."

I followed him and seated myself on the tailgate while he took beers out of a cooler. He gave me one, crossed over to Don and handed him one, then returned and sat next to me.

"Zahn said he'd send me a lady detective, but he didn't say she'd be such a pretty one."

"Well, thanks for the compliment."

"It's no compliment, just the truth." He swigged beer and looked appraisingly at me.

"Have you been a client of Hank's long?"

"Years, ever since he started the co-op. I knew him in 'Nam. He was an officer, I was an ordinary grunt. But Zahn always treated everybody like regular human beings. Rank didn't matter to him."

"Still doesn't. He even treats *me* like a human being."

"Shouldn't be so hard to do." He winked one of those incredibly blue eyes at me and drank more beer. "What did he tell you about my problem?"

"Nothing. Just said to call you."

"Yeah, and thanks for waiting until I could get back to you."

"Where was it I left the message anyway? The guy who answered said something about an oasis, but I didn't catch the rest. There was a lot of background noise."

"The Oasis Bar and Grill, on Irving Street. They take my messages."

"I see."

"To get to my problem: Somebody's been following me, and I want it stopped."

"Following you."

"Yeah. Watching my stall here at the flea market. And my house, where I've got this permanent garage sale. He isn't watching my people yet, but that's probably next."

"Your people?"

"The runners I send out to the other area flea markets. There are three of them."

I took out a pencil and notepad. "How long has this been going on?"

"About three weeks."

"How many people? One? More?"

"I've only noticed one."

"Can you describe him?"

He took off the cowboy hat and ran a hand through his curly hair. "He's weird."

"Weird?"

"Not one of the usual types."

"What usual types?"

"You know, the cops."

I gave him a puzzled look.

"The cops. They're always after me."

"Why?"

Now he looked confused. "Didn't Hank tell you?"

"Tell me what?"

"I'm a fence."

I stared at him, then glanced over at the coffeemakers and clock radios. "You mean you deal in stolen goods?"

"Sure. I don't broadcast it usually, but Zahn said I could trust you. I just figured he'd spelled it out."

Disturbed, I set the pencil and notepad down. While all my clients weren't necessarily on the right side of the law, I didn't hold much brief for fences. A couple of years ago I'd unmasked a ring of them operating in my former neighborhood, with tragic consequences. Fences, while not thieves themselves, encouraged thievery. And I'd often seen the heartbreak it could cause.

In my contract with All Souls I had the option of turning down jobs, providing the investigation wasn't related to a case we were handling. Knowing me as he did, Hank would have realized I would have reservations about working for a fence. So why hadn't he briefed me on Willie's occupation, as he normally would have on any sensitive detail about a client?

"And you say Hank's aware of what you do?"

"Of course; he's my lawyer."

I was amazed. The statement revealed a totally new aspect of my boss's character. Or did it? No matter how irrational they might seem on the surface, Hank usually had good reasons for his actions. If he'd sent me to see Willie, neglecting to mention his profession, there was more to this than was readily apparent.

Willie leaned toward me, frowning, as if he were worried that he had made a social blunder. "You're not shocked or anything?"

"Well . . . not really. It doesn't matter." But I would have to talk to Hank before I agreed to take Willie on as a client.

"Damn straight!" There was a touch of relief in the way he crumpled his beer can and tossed it under the truck. "I look at it this way: I may be a fence, but I've got rights just like the next guy. And I want this following business stopped."

I decided I might as well take down the preliminary information, so I picked up the notebook again. "Okay, describe the person."

"Weird, like I said. Little skinny guy. Wears glasses. Wears a suit."

"A suit, here at the flea market?"

"Yeah. It's no wonder I noticed him, huh?"

"I guess. Anything else?"

"A funny hat."

"How is it funny?" Carefully I avoided looking at Willie's leather cowboy hat with its braid and bright red feather.

"Sort of round—it fits close to the crown of his head. Like a beanie."

Quite improbably, it sounded like a Jewish *yarmulke*. "Anything else?"

He screwed up his face in concentration. "Not that I recall."

"Do you know anyone who might have reason to follow you? An enemy, for instance?"

"I deal tough, and sometimes it makes people mad at me, but I don't really make enemies."

"What about your merchandise—do you handle valuable items?"

"Well, some command high prices, but there's nothing like art goods or jewelry, if that's what you mean."

"And you don't deal in drugs?"

"No, ma'am."

"You owe any money? Gambling debts, perhaps?"

"Nope. I operate on a strictly cash basis, and I stay away from the tables and the track."

"Could it have any connection with a romantic relationship? A former girlfriend, for instance? Or an ex-wife?"

"Not that I can imagine. I got an ex-wife, but she's remarried twice now. Lives in another state. And my other women, I've always treated them right."

"Are you currently involved with someone?"

"Yeah, a little gal called Alida Edwards. She runs a handcrafted jewelry concession here."

"What does she think about this person who's been watching you?"

"She's as puzzled as I am."

"If you're so puzzled, why don't you go up and ask him what he's doing? You look as if you can take care of yourself."

He hesitated. "Look, I'm a fence. I'm in a vulnerable position. I don't want to do anything that might attract attention to me."

"Has the guy been around today?"

"No, but he might be waiting near the house when I get back. That's happened before."

"What time will that be?"

"Today I'll leave here around three. I've got a couple of truckers coming, wanting to peddle me some goods they've boosted."

"How about if I meet you there?" Until I could talk with Hank about Willie, I might as well follow up on his problem. And, for professional reasons, it might be helpful to watch a fence operate.

"Sure." He gave me his address, in San Francisco's inner Sunset district, near Golden Gate Park and Kezar Stadium.

I finished my beer and then rejoined Don. He was regarding the bathtub critically. "The enamel's shot. You'd do better at a junkyard if you want one of these things."

"Probably. But I'm not sure I do want one."

He reached out and smoothed down my hair. "For a new home-owner, you're pretty cavalier about getting the place in shape."

"Yes, I am, aren't I?" Much as I loved my new home, there were a great many things that interested me more—including Willie Whelan's problem.

chapter two

I dropped Don off at my house and then drove across town to the address Willie had given me. It was on the section of Arguello Boulevard that stretches between Kezar Stadium and the University of California Medical Center, on the fringes of Golden Gate Park. The neighborhood serves as home for an odd mixture of middle-class professionals, students from the Med Center, and bohemian types who spill over from the nearby Haight-Ashbury. While most of the buildings seem well-maintained, the mouldering shell of long-abandoned Polytechnic High School and the crumbling stadium cast a seedy pall over the area.

I parked and got out of the car, looking for signs of the man Willie had described, but saw no one remotely resembling him on the street. Then I crossed toward my prospective client's house, a stucco-and-beam Edwardian that had probably been built around the turn of the century. It was three stories, with the main floor several steps up from the sidewalk, and a garage underneath. As I approached, I saw that the garage door was up, and I glimpsed Willie standing just inside of it. He waved and motioned for me to come in.

The garage took up the entire basement and must have been close to a thousand square feet. Its walls were lined floor to ceiling with merchandise on makeshift plywood shelving. A long clothes rack held expensive-looking suits, coats, and dresses. Most of the goods on the shelves—small appliances, housewares, TVs, video recorders, cameras, and sound equipment—was new and still in the original packaging, but I spotted a group of more interesting older things—other pedestal sinks, some stained-glass panels, an ancient pinball machine, and a Victrola.

Two men in work clothes—presumably the truckers Willie had mentioned—were sitting on a pair of mismatched kitchen chairs in the space where a car would normally have been parked. When I entered, they stood up, shuffling their feet and glancing warily from me to Willie. He held up a hand and said, "Relax. She's okay," and they returned to their seats.

To me, Willie added, "I've still got some dealing to do. Look around, why don't you?"

I nodded and, marveling at the quantity and variety of merchandise, wandered off toward the back of the garage. While the light up front came from fluorescent fixtures, here it was filtered through two wire-mesh-covered windows that looked out on a yard. I glanced through them and saw a sun-parched lawn and crumbling cement birdbath. There was a cluttered desk to one side of the window, and a two-year-old Japan Airlines calendar—a feeble attempt at decoration—on the wall above it. Next to the desk stood an old refrigerator, its motor wheezing and grunting as if it might give up the effort at any moment. I stood and examined the costume jewelry in a glass case that separated the office area from the rest of the garage, listening to Willie's conversation with the truckers.

"Yeah, Joey, these suede jackets are nice. Real nice. But it's hotter than the hinges of hell out there. Who's gonna buy a suede jacket in this heat?"

"In the fall—"

"Sure, in the fall. Then they'll move. But in the meantime, I got a dozen jackets laying around here taking up space."

"Willie, that's top-quality suede."

"I'm not questioning the quality. I'm saying I can't move them now. Bring them back, maybe in a couple of months. Then we'll talk."

"I can't keep hot jackets around the house for two months! The wife would—"

"I can't keep them around either. Not at the price you're asking. Ties up too much of my capital." There was a long pause. "Tell you what I *can* do: I can take them off your hands for half of what you're asking."

"Aw, come on, Willie!"

"It's the best I can do. I don't know, Joey, maybe you can find somebody else who's willing to tie up his money in out-of-season goods. If I were you, I'd give it a try."

The man was silent. Then Willie spoke to the other. "How many of these cameras you got, Jim?"

"Six more in the truck."

"Japanese, huh? Nikon, that's a good brand. But look here, Jim: there's part of it missing."

"What the hell do you mean? That's the way they shipped them, right from the factory."

"Well, maybe they screwed up. This camera's not all here. See this gizmo? Where you put the flash? It's not there. If the flash isn't there, it don't work right. How's somebody supposed to take pictures inside if there's no flash?"

"Jesus, Willie, I've got *seven* of these."

"Yeah, seven cameras that don't work."

"They go for hundreds in the stores."

"Right—but those have got all the parts."

"I'll never unload them—"

"Tell you what. A hundred bucks for the lot."

"I thought you said they was no good."

"They're not." Willie's voice became elaborately patient. "But I see a lot of stuff come through here; maybe someday I'll see a flash attachment for one of these. Maybe not. It's a long shot, but I'm willing to bet a hundred bucks on the off chance that someday a flash attachment will come through that door."

"I don't know. I'd hoped to get—"

"Well, you can quit hoping. Nobody's going to pay big bucks for a camera that's not all there."

The man sighed. "Okay. I'll go get the others."

"Do that. I'll write you up a receipt." Willie started back toward the office, then stopped and snapped his fingers. "Oh, yeah. Joey, what about those jackets? You want to unload them for half price?"

"Guess I got no choice."

"I'll do up a receipt for you too." Willie went around the jewelry counter, winking at me, and pulled two Budweisers from the refrigerator. He took them to the man, saying, "Have a beer and give one to Jim when he comes back." Then he returned to the desk and busied himself with a receipt book and a check register. The men joined him; receipts were signed, checks were endorsed, cash changed hands, and the truckers left. I watched the entire procedure, unable to make much sense of it.

After the truckers were gone, I said, "Willie, I have a Nikon camera. They work perfectly well without flash attachments."

He grinned and took out two more beers. "I know."

"They never come equipped with flash attachments. You buy them separately."

"Yeah, but old Jim don't know that." He opened a beer and handed it to me. "He's what you might call ignorant."

"You tricked him."

"Sure I did. Dealt him right out of a nice profit."

"What about the other guy—Joey? Will those jackets really sit here for two months?"

"Hell, no. I'll have them at the flea markets tomorrow. They'll be gone in an hour."

"You're quite a businessman."

"It's all in the wheeling and dealing. Wheeling and dealing." His voice was flat, as if the transactions had given him a high and he was now coming down from it. "Let's go have a seat up front."

I followed him up there and took one of the mismatched kitchen chairs. Willie closed the garage door with an automatic control and slumped next to me.

"I take it the fellow in the suit wasn't out there when you got back?" I asked.

"Not today, for a change."

I sipped beer for a moment, trying to accommodate myself to his sudden change in mood. Finally I said, "Can I ask you some questions?"

"Fire away."

"They probably won't seem like they have much to do with your problem, but I need to get a feel for your business before I decide how I can help you."

"That's okay."

"You gave those two men receipts, wrote them checks, and then also paid them in cash."

"Right."

"What's all that supposed to accomplish?"

"Keeps the law off my back. In case you get caught with hot stuff, what you need is a receipt and a canceled check. That proves you thought you were buying legitimate."

"If the merchandise is hot, what does it matter what you thought?"

"Because to convict a person of receiving, they've got to prove he knew the stuff was stolen."

I remembered Hank telling me something to that effect once. "So you write up a receipt. Not in the person's real name, I assume."

"Nope. And the check's the same way."

"Then how can he cash it?"

"He doesn't. I pay him in cash. He endorses the check with the fake name. And I just take it to my bank and deposit it right back in one of my accounts. Then, if the cops come around, I got a receipt and a canceled check, all legal."

"Sounds complicated."

"It is. But it works."

"I guess you do a pretty good business."

"It's a living."

"How'd you get started?"

"In a small way. And then it got bigger."

I sensed that was all I would get out of him, so I went off onto another tack. "Do people like those truckers—"

"Thieves, you mean."

"Well, yes, thieves. Do they come here any time they feel like it?"

"There's a pattern to it. Early in the morning, I'm usually down here by seven. By ten I've done most of my buying. Then I take it easy, wait for people to see the 'garage sale' sign and drop in. Some of the stuff I buy comes from shoplifters. *They* start coming in around one-thirty, two, after they've worked the stores over the noon hour. That's when they get crowded and security is lax."

I'd once worked as a department store security guard and I re-membered those hectic noon hours all too well. Most shoplifters I'd apprehended during the day were kids or frustrated house-wives—people you really had to feel sorry for on a certain level. But the professional thieves who operated during the peak hours—they were hard cases and, as far as I was concerned, deserved tougher sentences than the courts handed out to them.

Again I felt a twinge of conscience at even contemplating help-ing Willie, but I had to admit I was fascinated. "So your thieves pretty much keep to normal business hours?"

"With me they do. Oh, when I was first in the business they'd come around any time—two, three in the morning even. If I didn't answer the door, they'd stand on the sidewalk and holler, toss stones at my bedroom window. I put a stop to that fast—after all, I got my reputation with the neighbors to consider."

Willie looked thoughtful, scratching his curly head. "I guess you could say I'm quieting down in my old age," he went on. "There was a time when I'd do anything to turn a profit. But now, I don't know. I don't need to prove anything anymore. I mean, I know I'm good."

I glanced around the garage. "I guess you must be."

He sat up straighter, his enthusiasm returning. "I'll tell you—a good fence is somebody who can move merchandise. I've handled just about any kind of goods you can name in my day; I can get rid of anything. But you know what? There's no thrill in it anymore.

Oh sure, dealing like you heard me do with those truckers gives me a lot of satisfaction. But it don't last, not like it used to. Hell, more and more I find myself making a legitimate deal just because it's easier." He glanced sidelong at me, as if he had just admitted a minor perversion and was afraid I would be shocked.

"I wouldn't worry about it," I said mildly.

"Okay, so now you tell me this: How are you going to stop this guy who's following me?"

I was about to say I wouldn't know if I was going to take his case until I spoke with Hank, but something stopped me. This was intriguing, dammit. Willie Whelan could provide me with an entrée into a world I'd never see otherwise. And the knowledge I'd gain might be useful in solving future cases; after all, wasn't it better to know how the other side operated? "How would you like to take on a new employee?"

"Huh?"

"You say you have three runners—why not add another?"

"You mean you'd pose as one and check things out?"

"Right. It's better if no one knows who I am, even your other people."

Willie studied me, then nodded decisively. "That might work. You can come along with me tomorrow to the flea markets and I'll show you the ropes. I'll tell my runners I'm training you to handle the Berkeley Flea Market—I don't have anybody there."

"Good."

He went to open the garage door. "I leave early. You'll have to be here at seven."

"No problem."

Willie accompanied me to the driveway, stopping to kick at the tire of his truck, which was parked in front of the house. It was still loaded with the merchandise I'd seen at the flea market, including the parrot and the player piano.

"Isn't it a lot of trouble, lugging a piano around?" I asked.

"Damn right it is. I only do it because I'm trying to unload it fast. It's taking up too much space for what it's worth."

"No luck, huh?"

"Hell, no. I've been dragging it all over for a month now." He stared at the piano, his mood pensive again. "And wouldn't you know it? It just had to be."

"Had to be what?"

"I took that piano in a legitimate deal. Wouldn't you know?"

chapter three

My new house was on a one-block segment of Church Street, out past Thirtieth, where the J streetcar tracks turn and come to an end. The street was not properly in my old neighborhood, the Mission district, nor was it in the newly fashionable area called Glen Park. If anything, it had a character all its own—one growing out of the blend of races and social classes that lived there in peaceable and friendly proximity. After only three months, I'd been made to feel I was a welcome addition to the tiny community.

The house itself was a five-room brown-shingled structure nestled between two larger Victorians. One of some four thousand cottages built by the city's Earthquake Relief Corporation to house homeless victims of the 1906 'quake, it had originally been a dark green three-room box without any claim to distinction. Over the years, however, a succession of owners had added the shingles, a front and rear porch, two additional rooms, and indoor plumbing. The toilet was in a cold cubicle on the back porch, and the living room ceiling was caving in, but as soon as I saw the house I fell in love with it. And before the then-owners had even accepted my offer, I'd rushed to the library to read up on the earthquake cottages.

As almost every San Franciscan knows, the 'quake and fire of April 18, 1906, left at least half of the city's 450,000 residents homeless. At first the people improvised, living in makeshift camps on vacant lots or in the parks, but the foggy summer weather soon made it apparent that there had to be a more permanent solution to the housing problem. It was then that the Relief Corporation stepped forward with its plan for the cottages—two rooms, some three, and none costing over a hundred and fifty dollars to construct. Soon teams of horses could be seen pulling the little green houses to their final destinations on empty land all over the city. Mine had been hauled to Church Street, and there it had sat on its deep pine-shaded lot, waiting for me to find it some seventy years later.

Now as I got out of my car and approached the front steps, I smiled at the house, pointedly ignoring the fact that the pitched roof was badly in need of repair. On the porch, behind the pot of geraniums I'd set out, was my cat Watney. He'd taken to hiding there and spying on the activity in the street—a ridiculous ploy, since the black-and-white spotted creature was so fat it would have taken a redwood tree to camouflage him adequately. As I put my key in the lock, he leapt out, nipped at my ankle, and then darted through the door in front of me. I followed him as he sashayed proudly back to the kitchen. Of course, Watney thought I'd bought the house for him.

All five rooms were empty, but there was a big pot simmering on the stove. I lifted the lid and smelled tomatoes, onions, garlic, oregano, and other less definable spices. It had to be one of the wonderful Italian sauces that were Don's specialty. I looked out the window and spotted him in a lounge chair under the big pine at the back of the yard. The sight of him flooded me with a warm, homey feeling—one I'd been experiencing with increasing frequency since he'd come to visit a week ago.

I responded to Watney's pleas for food, then got myself a glass of white wine, wondering, as I did every time I went into the refrigerator, why it was my fate to be plagued with strange appliances. In my last apartment, I'd had an old electrified icebox that didn't keep things very cold. This house had come equipped with a bright yellow 'fridge on which someone had painted racing stripes. It froze everything.

Before I went to join Don in the yard, I picked up the phone and tried to call Hank at All Souls. The phone there rang seven times before one of the attorneys answered, and then there was so much noise in the background that I could barely hear him. They were having a party, he said. Did I want to come over?

"What are you celebrating?" I asked.

"Well, today's the day back in 1952 that Lillian Hellman refused to squeal on her associates before the House Committee on Un-American Activities."

"What?"

"It really is."

"Oh." I realized he must be standing next to the literary calendar that someone had posted in the kitchen. "Is Hank there?"

"No. He went to Bodega Bay for the weekend. Guess he doesn't like Lillian Hellman."

"Probably not. If you see him, tell him I'll talk to him on Monday."

"Are you coming over?"

"I don't think so." I wasn't in any mood for a drunken crowd.

"Don't like Hellman either, huh?"

"She's okay, but I prefer Dashiell Hammett." I hung up and took my wine to the backyard.

By coincidence, Don was reading a novel by another mystery writer—Ross Macdonald, whose work I enjoyed even more than Hammett's. He set it down on the spool table between the two lounge chairs when I came out.

"I got you hooked, didn't I?" I sat down and nodded at the book. Mysteries were practically all I read these days, with the exception of an occasional foray into my old field, sociology. As I got older and further removed from college, however, the Soc books tended to sit face down on the coffee table, open to one of the first ten pages, gathering dust.

"Yeah, you have. I only meant to read for a little while and then light the barbecue, but . . ."

"We're barbecuing tonight?"

"I thought we would."

"So what's that in the pot on the stove?"

"Barbecue sauce."

"*Italian* barbecue sauce?"

"Sure. You don't expect a Del Boccio to cook like a Texan, do you?"

Again the homey warmth spread through me, this time tinged with unease. I'd have to examine this feeling more carefully sometime when I was alone. Was I really ready for . . . ?

". . . surprises me that a private eye would want to read about fictional ones," Don was saying.

"What?"

"I mean, don't mystery novels seem pretty unrealistic to you?"

"That's what I like about them. They're so much more interesting than my life. When you spend a lot of your time interviewing witnesses and filing documents at City Hall, you appreciate a little excitement on paper."

"Your life hasn't been *that* dull. How did it go with Willie?"

"Not bad. I'm going to take the case."

"I thought you didn't like the idea of working for a fence."

"Willie's no ordinary fence. And his problem intrigues me."

"What he told you sounded pretty run-of-the-mill to me."

"It's what he didn't tell me."

"Such as?"

"Well, consider Willie: He deals with tough customers every

day. He's tough himself. From the looks of him, I'd say he can handle most things that come along."

"So?"

"So somebody's following him. A little guy in a suit. If a little guy in a suit were bothering you, what would you do?"

"Go up and ask him what the hell he's doing."

"Right. So would I. But why doesn't Willie? This guy has been bugging him for three weeks, by his account. And has Willie once approached him, tried to find out what's going on? No. Instead, he calls his lawyer and hires a private detective. Why?"

"Did you ask him?"

"Yes. He said that as a fence he's vulnerable, doesn't want to get into anything that will call attention to himself."

"But you don't believe that?"

"I'm not sure. It could very well be true, but on the other hand, it might not be."

Don got up and went to the barbecue. I watched him, liking the way he moved. He was a stocky man, but he handled himself with confidence and a certain grace. Don had dark Italian good looks that had attracted me immediately when we'd met last fall while I was on a case in his hometown of Port San Marco. I hadn't been sure how we'd get on otherwise, however, because he was a disc jockey—star of the most raucous, nerve-jangling rock show on the mid-coast airwaves. Then I'd found out that he did most of his show wearing earplugs; that he loved Brahms and Tchaikovsky; that he adored salami and cheese and rich red wine. Most important, Don could laugh at himself.

"Anyway," I went on, "I've decided to take the case, but that means canceling our plans for brunch tomorrow. I have to be at Willie's at seven in the morning, so I can go around to the flea markets with him."

Unperturbed, Don poured charcoal lighter on the briquettes. "That's okay. There's a free concert at Stern Grove that I wouldn't mind catching."

Another thing I liked about him was his self-sufficiency. Given the erratic hours and unpredictable demands of my job, I'd always assumed I wouldn't find a man who could put up with me. But now—well, maybe I had.

The fire was blazing nicely. Don came over and sat down. "Do you want to start replastering the living room ceiling tonight?" he asked.

I sighed. We'd stripped what plaster remained from the lath and prepared the surface. We'd bought the supplies and borrowed a scaffold. Tonight was the only time I had free to work on it. "No."

"What do you want to do?"

"I want another glass of wine."

"And then?"

"Another. And then lots of barbecued ribs. And then I want to go to bed early."

"How early?"

"No later than eight. I'll have to get up at six and they say you need at least eight hours' sleep."

Beneath his shaggy mustache, Don's mouth began to curve up. "Eight at night to six in the morning is ten hours."

"I know."

He winked at me. "I'll get you that glass of wine."

chapter four

The next morning, Willie and I got in the red truck at his house and headed south on 101 to the San Jose Flea Market. As we drove, I stared sleepily at the little businesses and cheap apartments on the frontage road. The Peninsula, bounded on the east by the Bay and on the west by mountains and then the sea, was a string of communities with names like Millbrae, San Carlos, Palo Alto, and Mountain View. From the freeway, one was indistinguishable from the other, and I'd often had the feeling that I was driving through the endless outskirts of a town that stubbornly refused to materialize. There ought to be someplace tangible here, with parks and houses and palm-lined streets; but instead there was mile after mile of fast food stands, shopping centers, termite exterminators, and convenience stores.

At first Willie was silent, drinking coffee from a plastic cup with a screw top that kept it from spilling. Then, as the caffeine perked him up, he started talking about the fencing business.

"I get terrific customers at my permanent garage sale, you know? Just terrific. I love 'em all. You wouldn't think there'd be much traffic where I am, practically out in the Avenues. But it's all word-of-mouth. One tells another, and then another. Pretty soon you've got a regular clientele."

"Like who?"

"Anybody. Other flea market vendors looking for merchandise, of course. Clerks from the stores down on Irving Street or over on Haight. Secretaries, I get a lot of secretaries—they don't get paid so good and they're always looking for a bargain. Tellers from the bank where I do business—they catch on to me fast. And the Medical Center—Jesus Christ, doctors are the cheapest bastards alive. I got this one last week, drives up in a silver-gray Lincoln, leaves the goddamn thing right in the driveway so people have to squeeze around it. Suits he wants, designer suits. I show him where his size is, and next thing he's upset because they don't still have the labels in them. How's he supposed to know whether it's a Cardin or Yves St. Laurent?

"I tell him he wants labels he should go downtown to Brooks Brothers. He doesn't like that much, but he quiets down, decides to try some on. I show him the place I got curtained off at the back of the garage. He wants to know why there's no full-length mirror. *Then* he wants alterations. I say, 'Do I look like a seamstress?' When the guy finally leaves, he's got two designer suits for around a hundred bucks. Not a bad deal, but he's still annoyed and when he goes to back out of the driveway, he knocks over my garbage can that I've got sitting there, all full of crap that I've got to scrape up off the sidewalk with my bare hands.

"I tell you, it's not easy sometimes. But I still love my customers, every one of them, whether they're at the garage sale or the flea market. I move a lot of stuff through the markets, now that I've got three runners. I go around, check on each of them, then go to the Saltflats and get myself a little fresh air and sunshine, make some deals.

"Now, this market we're going to first in San Jose, it's more commercial than the Saltflats. You'll see. They got an office that's open all week, a lot of permanent vendors, food concessions. And they play it straight with the law; you got to be careful that anything you sell there has a legitimate-looking pedigree. Real careful, because you don't want a run-in with management or the San Jose cops. . . ."

The drive passed quickly and soon we were parking in a rutted lot across the street from the market. As Willie had said, it was more substantial than the Saltflats, with permanent booths and bins for the regular vendors to store their merchandise in. Most of the sellers were just setting out their goods, and many waved and called to Willie as he strode by with me in tow. We passed hot dog stands and popcorn wagons and *tacquerías* before we came to the displays of cheap clothing, garish ceramics, and tacky furniture.

Willie led me through the maze to a stall near its center, saying, "The guy that's snooping around won't be here because they're not letting the customers in yet, but I wanted you to get an idea of the setup. Here we are." He motioned at a beefy, balding man in his mid-forties who was stringing *piñatas* on an overhead wire. "And that there's my San Jose runner, Roger Beck."

The man glanced over his shoulder. His face was round and puffy, and on his thick forearms were tattoos of anchors. "Be right with you, Willie." He clipped a brightly colored papier-mâché donkey to the wire, which sagged under the added weight.

"Lots of Mexs come here," Willie said, "so we stock the kind of crap they like."

Roger Beck let the wire sag and came toward us, wiping his hands on his khaki pants. "How you doing, Willie?"

"Not bad, for a Sunday. Rog, this is Sharon McCone, newest member of the team. She's going around with me today, learning the ropes. Then I'm going to turn her loose on the Berkeley Flea Market. Anything you can fill her in on will help."

Beck's eyes, pinpoints in his fleshy face, turned slowly to me. "You hired a woman?"

"Why not? I'll take on anybody who can handle the job."

"Yeah, but can she? It's a rough business, especially for a broad. And that Berkeley market's weird."

"This lady can take care of herself." There was a cold edge to Willie's voice that seemed out of proportion to Beck's sexist but fundamentally harmless remark. I glanced uneasily at him.

To me, Willie said, "Rog's what you call your basic male chauvinist. Doesn't like women much, especially since his old lady took off with an insurance salesman and the family silverware."

Roger Beck's face flushed and he turned back to the *piñatas*, jerking angrily on the wire.

"Since then," Willie went on, "he drives a bakery truck during the week and moonlights for me on Saturdays and Sundays. It's not much, but it helps pay the bills the old lady left. And he fits right in here, with all the other rednecks."

I frowned.

"You see, Sharon, this is real redneck territory. Guns on the racks of the pickups. Shit-kicking music. Law and order, beer and pretzels, touch-my-woman-and-I'll-kick-your-ass. You're in for a real treat."

There was silence as Beck pulled the wire taut. Then he turned and said with tightly controlled anger, "There anything you want me to get out of the truck?"

"Yeah. Half a dozen suede jackets. A carton of sweaters—bright colors, the Mexs'll love them. Some socket sets. Receipts are all in the glove compartment; take them in case you need them."

Willie handed him his key ring and the beefy man left the stall, his big fists balled at his sides.

"You were rough on him," I said.

"Yeah, I guess I was." He was looking thoughtfully after Beck.

"Do you usually ride him like that?"

He turned abruptly, motioning for me to follow him. "Look, don't worry about it. Nothing I say really bothers Rog. Doesn't bother him at all."

But it did, and Willie knew it. I suspected the fence wasn't exactly a cheerleader for women's rights, so it couldn't have been Beck's remark that set him off. And he didn't strike me as a gratuitously cruel man. There had to be more going on between him and Beck than he was willing to discuss. The unpleasant scene kept puzzling me as Willie led me around, introducing me to other vendors and explaining the workings of the market.

The next flea market Willie took me to was on Alameda Island, a stone's throw from Oakland. It was on the grounds of a drive-in theater near the Naval Air Station, and didn't seem nearly as commercial as the San Jose operation. Even the vendors were more low-key as they lounged in the sun, watching the first customers straggle by. I caught snatches of conversation as Willie led me toward his stall near the drive-in's snack bar.

". . . so I told him if he wants me to take this literary crap that nobody buys, at least he could give me a price break on the good stuff—coffee-table books, you know? But a lot of good that does me. . . ."

". . . big dealers, they're all alike. Don't give the little guy nothing. . . ."

". . . like I told my daughter, I come for the sun. You can go crazy in a dingy windowless store six days a week. . . ."

". . . some party and, believe me, I could use a few aspirin right now . . ."

". . . a sale's a sale . . ."

". . . looking for antiques?" The words were addressed to me this time. The old man stood amidst a motley collection of rickety tables, hideous lamps, and tattered mattresses. I stopped, staring at the fattest, ugliest overstuffed chair I'd ever seen.

"Plenty of genuine antiques here."

I started to move on.

"Mainly me," the man added.

I smiled at the joke and hurried to catch up with Willie.

He was waiting impatiently in front of a stand that sold jeans and T-shirts. When I came up, he took a firm hold on my arm and propelled me down the aisle. "That's my stand up ahead, with the barber pole in front. Nobody watching it; I guess he hasn't started in on my runners yet."

I glanced around; he seemed to be right.

The wares in this stall were different from those at San Jose, I noted. There was no clothing or *piñatas*, but instead a few antiques, some serviceable-looking furniture, housewares, and a great many children's toys. When I commented on it, Willie said, "You stock to fit the clientele. Here you get a lot of young families who shop seriously. They want top value for their dollar."

The words reminded me of an earnest young marketing executive I'd once known, and briefly I wondered to what heights Willie might have risen if he'd entered business school instead of becoming a fence.

A rail-thin man in a T-shirt that showed the outlines of his ribs was unloading a tricycle from the battered van parked at the back of the space. He set it down, paused to take a swig from a beer can that rested on the van's bumper, then trundled the trike over to a group of strollers. His movements were slow, almost trancelike. When he turned, I saw that he was in his middle thirties—and that some of those years must have been hard ones indeed. The most recent evidence of it was a black eye and raw abrasions on his face.

"Hey, Willie." He raised a hand.

"Morning, Sam. What the hell happened to you?"

The man ambled over to us, his thumbs hooked in the loops of his belt, looking sheepish. "It's nothing."

"Doesn't look like nothing to me. You seen a doctor?"

"Look, I'm okay."

"Yeah." Willie's tone was flat, disbelieving.

The man went back to his van, finished off the beer, and immediately pulled another from a paper sack.

"Bad night?" Willie asked.

"Carolyn left. Again."

"And?"

"She said she was going to stay with some friend on the Peninsula. So I went looking for her. Ended up in a bar in Hayward—"

"Hayward's not on the Peninsula, Sam."

"Shit, you think I don't know that? I was blind drunk, man. Anyway, I got in a fight, these two guys jumped me, and next thing I'm coming to in the parking lot." He shook his head and swigged beer.

"Yeah. Sam, this is Sharon. She's going to handle the Berkeley market for me. Sharon, Sam Thomas."

Sam looked at me with faint surprise, as if he hadn't been fully aware of my presence. "Hi, Sharon." To Willie, he said, "Glad you finally found somebody who'd go there."

Willie glanced at me, amused. "None of my runners want to work the Berkeley Flea Market. Too ethnic for them. Too many weirdos and liberals. You know Berkeley."

Sam took out another beer. "Well, it *is* weird. They've even got a chiropractor operating there, for Christ's sake. And the food— you ever had a tofu burger?"

"Speaking of food . . ." I began.

Willie looked at his watch. "Yeah, it's almost lunchtime. The fried chicken at the snack bar's not bad." He took out his wallet, extracted a twenty, and handed it to Sam. "Get us some, will you? And feed yourself, too."

"I'm not hungry." But he took the bill and shambled off, still clutching the beer.

"Does he always drink that much?" I asked.

"Yes." Willie was surveying the space with a critical eye. He went over and pushed the strollers closer to the van, then lugged a kitchen table out and piled some cookware on it. "Sam can never get it through his head how I want things arranged."

"So why do you put up with him? He's obviously an alcoholic.

Was it his wife who walked out last night?"

"His lady. But she'll be back, probably be there when he gets home tonight. Sam can get violent—it happens that way with some Vietnam vets—but it doesn't last long. When something sets him off, Carolyn leaves. But she's always come back—so far." In spite of his optimistic words, his eyes were troubled.

"She must love him, then. And you must like him pretty well, too."

"Let me tell you about Sam. Like I said, he's a Vietnam vet. Former Special Forces type. Went over there gung-ho. He wasn't like me—just an ordinary grunt who was too dumb to try to get out of it. Or like our friend Zahn, who was ROTC and went because he thought it was right, then came back to grow his hair and carry a protest sign. Sam really *believed* in that war.

"So he went over there and, like Zahn and me, he saw some pretty unspeakable things. Probably did some of them, too. But he didn't come home and forget like I did. Or try to change things like Zahn. He came home and remembered—too damn well. The booze kind of takes the edge off of it."

"And that's why you put up with him."

"I may be dumb about a lot of things, but I'm not too stupid to know that a lot of the cripples left over from 'Nam aren't in wheelchairs."

When Sam came back from the snack bar, he had a fresh six-pack and baskets of fried chicken for Willie and me. We sat in the van and talked—about the flea markets, about the Oakland A's and their chances this season, about where you could buy the cheapest gas. I don't know how Willie did it, but by the time we left, he'd convinced Sam to see a doctor about his face, at Willie's expense, of course. Sam should think of it as health insurance, he said. After all, didn't nearly everybody else in the world have Blue Cross these days?

That afternoon we drove across the Richmond Bridge to the Marin City Flea Market. On a vacant lot beside the freeway, it was even more low-key than Alameda. The stalls spread out haphazardly in all directions, and the wares they offered were more exotic than mundane. Willie and I checked for suspicious strangers, but again everything seemed normal.

Willie's Marin runner, Monty Adair, presented a marked contrast to his laid-back surroundings. Adair was angular and intense. His dark brown hair was cut military-style; his bright eyes snapped; his small nose and chin were sharply pointed. When he spoke, it was in short, clipped sentences.

"Nice to have you aboard, Sharon. Willie, there's a guy who wants to see you. He's in the third space, back aisle. Wants to know if you'll take a TV in trade for a car stereo. I said I'd send you by."

Willie nodded and left me in Adair's seemingly capable hands.

"So you're going to handle the Berkeley market?"

"Yes."

"It's different from Marin." He motioned at the crowd of people, mainly dressed in jeans and T-shirts, that drifted by. "Berkeley's eccentric. Marin's basically conservative."

I raised my eyebrows as a woman who appeared to have wrapped herself in a madras bedspread came up and began to root through a box full of books.

"Oh, some of them dress strangely. Marin County has a reputation for being on the forefront of social change. They feel they have to live up to it. But underneath they're conservative as they come. They care a lot about money. Houses. Cars."

A second woman came up. "You've got a rocker over there marked fifteen dollars. I'll give you ten."

"Sorry. Prices as marked."

The woman frowned and walked off.

"She'll be back," Adair said. "She can afford the fifteen. Those were designer jeans she had on." He turned to me. "That's one thing you have to remember, Sharon. You don't owe these people a thing. They're all out to screw you. Take my advice and screw them first."

The woman was circling the rocker, her eyes narrowed.

"This is a tough business," Adair went on. "Everybody wants something for nothing. I turn a good profit here by keeping prices firm. There's money in this county, and I get my share of it."

The woman gave the rocker a final appraising glance, then came back, rummaging in her purse. She handed Adair three crumpled five-dollar bills and said, "I'll be back for it in half an hour."

He took the bills without a thank-you and went to attach a "sold" tag to the chair. "Always tag things you're holding for a buyer. It's good psychology. Tells people your goods are moving."

"You're certainly giving me an education." I sat down on a folding chair.

"I'll give you another pointer. Not for today; you're not really working. But when you are, never sit down. It gives the impression you don't care if you make a deal."

"You should write a how-to book on this."

"Why? It would only help the competition." He smiled, but his eyes were dark brown stones.

"How long have you been at this?"

"Five years."

"Longer than Willie's other runners, then?"

"No, about the same. What made you think that?"

"They don't seem nearly as expert."

"They're not. Beck's basically a truck driver. Strong but stupid. Sam Thomas—have you met him?"

"Yes."

"Then you know." He paused, lighting a cigarette. "You could make something of that Berkeley market, Sharon."

"I hope to."

"You been over there yet?"

"No."

"It's in the parking lot of the Ashby Avenue BART station. They don't charge to get in. You're ahead right there. The customers—a lot of blacks. Berkeley oddballs. College students. Hangers-on. You know how Berkeley is."

"Actually I do. I went to school there."

"When?"

"Oh, around ten years ago."

"You get in on all that Communist ruckus?"

"The war protests? Some. I was too late for the Free Speech Movement."

"Do any protesting yourself?"

"Good Lord, no. I was too busy working so I could stay in school." I'd often marveled at how I could have gotten through four years at Cal without so much as heaving a bottle or a rock, but the years had passed in a steady rhythm of classes, work, more classes, and more work. Oh, I'd participated in the usual heated discussions over coffee or cheap wine. I'd signed petitions and watched the body count with growing horror and wept when a high school friend had died in shelling at Cam Rahn Bay. But sometimes I wondered if I shouldn't have done more. Would it, in some small way, have helped. . . ?

"Working at what?" Adair asked.

"Odd jobs." Actually I'd been a security guard, but he didn't need to know that.

"And now what do you do?"

"I'm a messenger for a bunch of lawyers."

"Does it pay well?"

"No."

"Then remember what I said. You can make something of this business if you try."

"I will. Thanks for all the advice." I could see Willie ambling down the aisle, occasionally stopping to examine merchandise or talk to a vendor. He came up, looking from Adair to me with a curious expression that I couldn't read.

"You two have a nice talk?"

"Very good," I said. "Monty's a real fund of information."

"That he is." Willie smiled mechanically at Adair. "I never have to tell him a thing. He knows just what to do to turn a tidy profit."

Adair returned the smile, just as mechanically. Under their polite manner, I sensed a coldness between the two men, more subtle than the antagonism between Willie and Roger Beck. Why? I wondered.

There was silence for a moment, and then Willie turned to me. "You ready to go see my home base, the Saltflats?"

I stood up, relieved to be going. "I sure am."

As we walked down the aisle toward the entrance, I looked back at Adair. He was closing in on a youth who was practice-swinging a new metal tennis racket. The boy turned and smiled. Adair's answering grin was predatory, his white teeth gleaming like a shark's.

chapter five

When we drove into the Saltflats Flea Market, a man with an iron-gray crewcut came out of the shack that served as an office and started toward the truck.

"Mack Marchetti," Willie said. "Runs the place."

Marchetti was a big man and, even though he had to be in his mid-fifties, his body was trim and well-conditioned. I guessed he was a former athlete who had kept in shape; in his creased slacks and alligator shirt, he certainly resembled the retired sports figures you see in commercials for savings-and-loans or insurance companies.

"Does he own this land?" I asked, mentally computing the value of what had to be highly desirable acreage.

"No. Leases it from the owners. That'll end next year, when they build an office park to go with the marina." Willie motioned down the frontage road, where there was a new man-made lagoon and the rudiments of docks and slips. "And then there'll be one less free thing for folks to do on a Sunday afternoon."

Marchetti came up and leaned on the driver's side window. "Willie, where the hell have you been?"

"Checking my people at the other markets. I'm breaking in a new runner, so it took longer than usual. Why?"

"Because I been holding your space, and not without a lot of trouble. Got a new kid with a load of automotive supplies, can't understand why I've stuck him in this little bitty space where there's acres of room to his right. Seems he never heard of the king of the flea markets, who can show up any time he damn well pleases." Marchetti smiled, nastily.

"You fill him in about me?" Willie's voice had the same cold edge as when he'd spoken with Roger Beck. Marchetti was obviously another person the normally easygoing fence didn't care for.

"Oh, sure. Got to keep the legend alive, even if you never do show up until two."

"I'm paying for that space, Marchetti."

"Yeah. See you continue to." The flea market operator turned and stalked back to the shack.

I said, "He reminds me of a football coach, chewing out a player who's late for practice."

"Funny you should say so; that's what old Mack did up until a few years ago—coached high school football." Willie put the truck in gear and we rolled slowly down the aisles to the place where I'd found him the day before. As Marchetti had said, the next space over was stacked with cartons of motor oil, filters, batteries, and other parts. The skinny young fellow perched on a folding chair glared at us as we pulled up.

The commodities displayed over there were obviously hot. I said to Willie, "I've heard Marchetti has a reputation for letting a lot more illicit dealing go on here than they do at the other flea markets. Is that true?"

"Mack's pretty loose about it, yes. I'll unload things here that it might be risky to sell at San Jose, for instance. That's one reason I stopped going to the San Francisco market, over by the Cow Palace. Mack makes everything nice and easy."

We got out of the truck and Willie off-loaded the two worn Oriental rugs. I helped him spread them on the ground, then began removing smaller objects and placing them around, while Willie dragged out the heavier things. As we worked, I glanced at the other stalls and passersby, hoping to glimpse the man Willie claimed had been following him. All I saw were the usual buyers and sellers. When the stall was set up, we sat down on the tailgate of the truck and I said, "So where do we go from here? Are there people I should meet?"

"They'll be by. Like Marchetti said, I'm king of the flea market. I'll just sit here and hold court."

As if to prove his point, a plump young woman with dark hair piled high on her head materialized from behind the truck. She was carrying a sackful of dried banana chips, which she tossed to Willie.

"For you," she said. Her accent was Spanish, and pronounced.

"Sharon, this here's Selena Gonzalez. She sells dried fruit and nuts, plus olives and some mighty fine houseplants. Selena, Sharon's my new runner."

She turned to me. "Welcome to the world of the flea market."

"Thank you."

"How's it going today?" Willie popped a handful of banana chips into his mouth and offered the bag to me.

"So-so. I sell some of this, some of that, but the people are not willing to part with very much money. I think it is because of that *bastardo* in the White House." She sat down on the ground, arranging her voluminous red peasant skirt over her knees. "Willie . . . you have not had any more visitors?"

"No." He looked at me. "She's noticed the man I told you about."

"I see."

"He worries me," she said. "The way he watches, always staring with those little eyes. He is evil."

"Selena likes to exaggerate," Willie said. "It's partly her culture, and partly the fact she sees an Immigration man behind every tree."

"You would too if you were in my delicate position."

"She means she's an illegal alien."

"And what of it? Don't I have the right to go where I please?"

"As they explained the last time they threw you out, there are such things as national boundaries."

"Boundaries. Pooh. What are boundaries? Imaginary lines made up by people like that *bastardo*—"

"Selena's also very opinionated politically—especially for a non-citizen."

"You would do well to take more interest yourself. It is people like you that allow things like this trouble in Latin America to happen. You allow maniacs to be elected—"

"Stop!" Willie held up a hand. "I'm guilty; I admit it. Just don't lecture."

"Lecturing is good for you." Selena looked at me. "Do not take him too seriously. He is a child, like most men." She stood, smoothing her red skirt. "Come and see me, if you want a plant, or just to talk. I am down the aisle to the right."

"Thanks. I will." I watched her go, then said to Willie, "Did Immigration really throw her out?"

"Twice. But she always comes back. God knows how she does it, but she's as persistent as a bad case of the *turista*."

A young couple came up and began poking around the player piano. A gleam in his eye, Willie got up and went over to them. I sat, feeling the sun beat down on my head. Today I had remembered to dress coolly, but I should have thought to bring a hat. Down the aisle, I could see the knife vendor sitting behind his cases of wicked-looking weapons, the small striped umbrella over his head and a smile on his face.

Willie came back and slumped dejectedly against the tailgate. "Damn! I swear I'm never going to get rid of that white elephant."

"Why'd you buy it, anyway?"

"Pure weakness. My lady friend, Alida Edwards, makes the jewelry she sells. There was a guy with a nice selection of agate; she really wanted it, but she was short on cash. So I traded some tape decks for the stones, but that wasn't enough for him. The asshole knows me, and he knows Alida, and that means he knows I'm a fool for the woman. So he held out on the deal until I said I'd take the piano too. And I've been carting it around for a month now."

"Does it work?"

"Sure. There're even some rolls for it, although where they've got to I don't know. My garage is so full, I'm not sure what I've got in there these days. Speaking of Alida, I want to run over to her stall for a minute. Can you handle things here?"

"Sure."

"Be back shortly."

He wandered off and I sat waiting for customers. People drifted in and out, mostly to look at the player piano and try to get the parrot to talk, but no one wanted to buy anything. The people in the aisles moved listlessly, and most of the sellers sat back, not even bothering to hawk their wares. A somnolent mid-afternoon feeling descended on the market, and I slouched against the side of the pickup's bed. My eyes moved lazily to the popcorn stand across the way, where a man in a dark suit stood. . . .

He was eating from a bag of popcorn as he stared fixedly at the truck. If the popcorn was supposed to be protective coloration, it didn't work. No one could look more out of place at a flea market; in fact, the *yarmulke*, dark suit, and shiny black shoes suggested that he'd probably wandered in by mistake while looking for the synagogue.

I forced myself to remain slouched, studying him from under drooping eyelids. He was slight, not more than my own five foot six, had a narrow ascetic face, and couldn't have been more than twenty-five. Again I wondered why Willie had not approached him himself. Surely it would not have caused a scene; the man looked as if he would jump right out of those shiny black shoes if anyone so much as said boo to him.

As I watched, he finished his popcorn, crumpled the bag, and threw it into a nearby waste container. The swift motions alerted me, and I sat up straighter. The man's eyes met mine and then he turned on his heel. I jumped off the tailgate and went after him.

I hurried across the aisle, nearly stumbling over a child with a helium-filled balloon. The man disappeared around the popcorn stand. I went through the narrow space between it and a used clothing concession, then stopped at the edge of the next aisle. It was easy to spot the *yarmulke*-covered head some ten feet to the left. The man was walking purposefully, but not fast. I followed, also taking my time.

He stopped in front of a display of sunglasses, his thin face reflected darkly in their hundreds of shiny lenses. His hand reached for a pair of glasses, wavered, and fell to his side. He moved along the display, selected another pair, and tried them on in front of a mirror. As he adjusted them and bent down to get a better look, I realized he was checking me out in the glass. Quickly he straightened, dropped the sunglasses on the counter, and trotted off down the aisle.

I followed him, weaving through the casual strollers. He increased his pace, glancing back over his shoulder. A woman lugging an overstuffed satin pillow stepped into his path, and he ran into her, bouncing off her soft burden. She laughed, and the man whirled, then veered off toward the exit. He was moving fast now, and people were turning to look.

He cut straight through an open stall that sold ceramics, and I followed. Briefly I was aware of the vendor standing open-mouthed, a garish ceramic cake topped with strawberries in her hands. The man plunged into a crowd near an ice cream peddler and, my eyes fixed on him, I smacked into a woman in a long dress who wore five flowered bonnets piled on her head.

"Watch where you're going!"

"Sorry!"

"That's okay. You want to buy a hat?" I heard her last words over my shoulder as I sprinted toward the exit. The man was pushing around a line of people and heading for the frontage road.

He ran along beside the cars that were parked there, his shiny shoes slapping on the pavement. I raced after him. Near the half-finished marina, he came to a sudden stop and jumped into a beat-up brown sedan. When I got to it, he was frantically grinding the starter.

I reached through the driver's window and grabbed at the keys. He slapped my hand, got the car started, and stalled it. I pulled the keys from the ignition and backed up, bracing myself for a struggle. But the man gave a groan and flopped back against the seat, his eyes closed. Beads of sweat stood out on his forehead.

"Okay," I said, "who are you and why have you been watching Willie Whelan?"

He remained still for a moment. Then he brought his hands down on the steering wheel with a thump.

"Answer the question."

Slowly he opened his eyes and turned his head. "Who are you?"

"One of Whelan's employees. Now you answer *my* question."

"I don't have to tell you anything. Give me back my keys."

"No."

"Give them to me!"

"Uh-uh."

He tried to glare at me, but wasn't able to summon up much ferocity. His fingers began to drum on the steering wheel. "I told them this would happen," he said.

"Told who?"

"The committee. I told them I'm no good at this sort of thing; none of my training has prepared me—"

"What committee?"

He shook his head.

I stuck the keys in the pocket of my jeans, went around to the passenger side, and got in the car.

"What are you doing?" He shrank back against his door.

"Neither of us is going anywhere until you talk."

"Get out of my car!"

"No."

He fell silent, staring down at his hands. He'd put up a token resistance, but there was very little real fight in him.

"Look," I said, "I'm a detective. Whelan hired me because you've been bothering him. You can either talk to me, or to the cops. Take your pick."

He remained silent.

"What committee?" I asked again.

He looked up, his face flooded with anger and frustration. "The Torah Recovery Committee. I told them it was ridiculous, skulking around like some kind of double agent, and now look what's happened!"

"What's your name?"

"I don't have to tell you."

"Like I said, you can tell me or you can tell the cops."

"Oh, all right! It's Levin. Jerry Levin."

"And you're a member of this . . . Torah Recovery Committee?"

"Sort of an investigator for them."

And a poor sort at that, I thought. "Okay, Jerry, what have they hired you to investigate?"

"The Torahs . . . Maybe I'd better start at the beginning."

"I wish you would."

"Torahs are Jewish religious scrolls. . . ." He paused. "There's a lot of background; it's complicated."

"We have plenty of time."

He sighed, glancing at his watch.

"As you were saying . . ."

"The Torah Recovery Committee is an East Coast organization. It was formed a couple of years ago, in response to a rash of thefts from synagogues back there."

"Thefts of Torahs?"

"Yes. The scrolls disappear, and later they turn up in other synagogues around the country."

"You don't mean the other congregations are stealing them?"

"Oh, no. What happens is they buy them, not knowing they're stolen."

"I see. And your job is to find them and get them back?"

"Yes."

"Where does this tie in with Willie Whelan?"

"I'll come to that. Torahs are hand-copied parchment scrolls. They contain only the Hebrew words from the first five books of the Old Testament. But in 1982, a number of congregations instituted a practice of marking their Torahs with code symbols—in the margins, in invisible ink. The codes are registered so there's a record of ownership. When a congregation is considering buying a Torah, they're supposed to check under ultraviolet light for the code."

"Does it work?"

"Sometimes, but not all that well. A lot of them are too trusting to do it; some are afraid of offending the sellers. Also, many congregations don't want to mark their Torahs, even invisibly; they feel it's a kind of desecration."

"I see." But I still didn't understand what all this talk of religious scrolls had to do with Willie.

"Recently quite a few stolen Torahs have turned up in Bay Area synagogues," Levin went on. "Some were detected right off, and that alerted other synagogues, who checked those they'd already purchased. There have been at least a dozen cases, and God knows how many others haven't been uncovered."

"And Willie—"

"There are indications that the Torahs may have been moved through his operation."

"What indications?"

"I can't say. It might give away the identity of our informant. But I can tell you that Mr. Whelan probably has several Torahs in his possession right now."

"A Torah is parchment, wound around two large wooden pegs with handles at either end, right?"

"Yes."

I thought back to the jumble in Willie's garage. I'd seen nothing remotely resembling a Torah there, but that didn't mean much. Willie himself didn't know for sure what he had back there. "What happens when you find someone is in possession of a stolen Torah? Do you go to the police?"

"If we feel the person is a thief, yes."

"What about someone like Willie? Would you call the police or merely try to get the Torahs back?"

"All we really want is the Torahs. I understand Mr. Whelan has a large fencing business; I don't suppose one arrest would stop him."

"No, I don't think it would." I was silent for a moment. If Willie did indeed have the stolen Torahs, chances were he'd taken them in an odd deal, like the player piano. I doubted if fencing religious scrolls constituted a large part of his livelihood. "What if I can get the Torahs back for you and promise that Willie won't trade in them again?"

"I think I could promise in return that we wouldn't bother him anymore."

I nodded. "I'll have to talk to him, of course. But I don't think there will be any problem. You've been annoying Willie by watching him, and all he wants is for it to stop."

"We'd have no need to watch him, once the Torahs are returned."

"Good. Then shall we go back to the market and settle this right now?"

Levin glanced nervously at his watch. "I'm supposed to meet with Rabbi Halpert in fifteen minutes."

"Who's he?"

"Rabbi David Halpert; he's my advisor here in San Francisco."

I'd heard of David Halpert; he was active in a number of social causes. "All right. What about this? You keep your appointment with the rabbi, and I'll talk to Willie. Then we'll all meet at seven tonight."

"Where?"

I thought of Willie's house, and then of the bar that took his messages. "The Oasis Bar and Grill, on Irving Street."

Levin wrinkled his nose.

"Don't worry; it's a respectable place. Bring Rabbi Halpert, if it will make you feel more comfortable."

"Maybe I will." He held out his hand, palm up.

I stared at it.

"May I have my car keys?"

"Oh, sure." I dug in my pocket and gave them back to him. "Don't forget—seven o'clock."

"I won't. We're as anxious to straighten this out as you are."

chapter six

Willie was mystified by the story of the stolen Torahs.

"I wouldn't know a Torah if I tripped over one. And I sure as hell wouldn't fence religious stuff anyway. Jesus, I was brought up a Catholic; I got too much respect to do a thing like that."

"Well, some informant claims you have been."

"I'd like to get my hands on the son-of-a-bitch—"

"That kind of talk isn't going to help us. We don't even know who he is."

"So now what do we do?"

"I think we should keep our appointment with Jerry Levin. Maybe you can convince him to tell you who the informant is. Or you might be able to convince him you don't have the Torahs, and then he'll go away."

When I left the flea market a few minutes later, Willie was muttering angrily to the parrot. The bird sat on its perch, regarding him with calm beady eyes.

As I parked in front of my house, Don's antique gold Jaguar pulled up behind my battered MG. He jumped out, looking exceptionally cheery, then hoisted a sack of groceries. "That was good timing!" he called.

I waited for him on the steps. "How was the concert?"

"Great. I love Stern Grove—all those eucalyptus trees. . . . How was your day?"

"Confusing."

"You want to talk about it?"

"Not right now." I unlocked the door and went down the hall to the kitchen. "I want to relax; I have to go out again at seven."

"That's fine with me. We've got the fixings for a feast here." He patted the grocery bag. "There's salami and some anchovies with capers and mozzarella."

"Sounds wonderful." I cleared the Sunday paper off the table and got out glasses and a bottle of red wine. The fog had started billowing in over the hills, and I went to change into a heavy sweater. When I came back, Don had the food spread on the table and was pouring wine. He hummed happily, some lilting tune that they must have played at the concert.

"You're sure in a good mood." I sat down and began to cut the salami.

"I know. I ran into an old friend at the Grove."

"Oh? Who?"

"Tony Wilbur, a guy who used to work at KPSM." KPSM was the station in Port San Marco where he was a disc jockey. "Tony's up here now, program director at KSUN."

"KSUN—that's the station that calls itself 'the light of the Bay.'"

"Right."

"It's a rock station. Sort of like KPSM."

"Worse. Louder. It's pretty horrible."

"Does your friend like working there?"

"Loves it. He's a nut, like me." Don paused. He looked like a little kid who had spent all his allowance on your birthday present and couldn't wait another minute to give it to you. "Babe, there's a job open at the station. Tony wants me to apply for it."

I picked up my wineglass, then set it down again. "A job as a disc jockey?"

"Yes."

"Doing the kind of show you have now?"

"Yeah."

"I thought you hated that show."

"I do, but . . ." He shrugged.

"I'd think if you made a move, you'd want to get into something you'd like better. Like a job with a classical station."

"Babe, there aren't that many classical stations around. Or many jobs for d.j.'s, period. This is a bigger station, in a major metropolitan area. It's better exposure, and the pay would be higher."

"I see." I felt a prickle of annoyance with myself. Why was I being so unenthusiastic? I picked up my glass and raised it in a toast. "Well, here's to good luck. If you want the job, that is."

"I do." But there was an uncertain look in his eyes.

"Then I think it's wonderful." I sipped wine and winked at him, then felt even more annoyed with myself. I *never* winked at anyone.

With a relieved grin, he winked back.

"So," I said, "what do you have to do, go in for an interview?"

"First I have to give him my demo tape."

"Demo tape?"

"A sample tape of a show. For a d.j., it's like a résumé."

"Oh. How do you get one made?"

"I have one."

"You have one. You mean with you?" A strange, flat feeling was stealing over me.

"Yeah, I had one made before I came up here."

"Why?"

"Just in case."

"Just in case you ran into someone who offered you a chance at a job?"

Don frowned.

"I mean, were you planning to look for a job here?"

"Not really. I just had the tape made. . . ." His voice trailed off and he began to cut some mozzarella.

I was being horrible and spoiling all his pleasure. Why? I liked having Don around; I should be pleased he wanted to move to San Francisco. If he did, it wouldn't necessarily mean . . . I reached across the table and took his hand.

"I think it was a great idea to bring the tape with you. And it would be terrific if you got a job up here."

He set the cheese cutter down. "Do you mean that?"

"Of course. Can I listen to the tape?"

"Sure." His enthusiasm rekindled, Don got up and bustled into the bedroom to get the tape from his suitcase. And I sat there, an odd, hollow feeling in my stomach.

The Oasis was a country-and-western bar. When I entered, a bunch of urban cowboys were rolling dice for drinks, and Waylon Jennings's voice boomed from the jukebox. I spotted Willie at the back of the room, behind a potted palm that seemed to be the bar's only concession to its exotic name.

I got myself a beer from the bar, then joined my client. He nodded perfunctorily. "You're early."

"Only fifteen minutes." I hadn't wanted to stay at home after Don had played his demo tape. It was very good, and chances were he'd get the job. He had wanted to talk about the possibility, something I couldn't do with this inexplicable flat feeling growing inside me.

There was a leather pouch on the table in front of Willie. I motioned at it and said, "What's that for?"

"The weekend's profits."

"From the flea market, you mean?"

"All of them. Sunday night, my runners check in and we divvy up the take. Usually they come to the house, but I left a note on the door for them to meet me here. All of them except old Sam have been by."

"Do you really expect him?"

"Yeah, Sam'll make it. Maybe."

We fell silent. From the jukebox, some singer whose voice I didn't recognize was complaining about lost love and loose women.

"So what do you think?" Willie said. "Is this Levin guy giving you a straight story?"

"I think so. Unless you're an awfully good actor, it's hard to come across as confused and inept as he did." But as I said it, I closed my eyes, reviewing my encounter with Jerry Levin.

"Huh." Willie was silent again.

I looked at my watch. Five to seven.

"Willie!" A woman with long blond hair stuck her head through the leaves of the potted palm. I jumped in surprise. "Sam told me you'd be here." She looked at me, a quick, appraising glance.

"Hi, honey." Willie took her hand and pulled her out from behind the plant. She was tall and very slender, and the tight jeans and T-shirt she wore accentuated it. Her Nordic face was deeply suntanned, almost flawless, and free of makeup.

"This here's Alida Edwards, my lady," Willie said. "Honey, this is Sharon McCone, the detective I told you about." ·

The tight lines around her mouth relaxed. "Thought he was stepping out on me for a minute there." She grinned and reached across the table to shake my hand. "Appreciate what you're doing for Willie." Her accent was Southern—Texas, perhaps.

"You said Sam told you I was here?" Willie took his feet off the other chair and turned to scan the bar.

"Yeah. Ran into him over at your house. He'd seen your note."
She reached into her fringed leather purse and brought out a large
manila envelope. "Said for me to give you this."

"Damn! He's gone and taken his cut and split. Every week I tell
him to let me divide it up, and 'most every week he pulls something like this."

Alida put a hand on Willie's shoulder. "Sam wouldn't cheat
you, baby. He's just in a hurry to drink up his pay."

"Yeah, I know. But his arithmetic isn't so hot sometimes."
Willie stuffed the envelope into the pouch and sat back, propping
his feet on the chair again. "So what're you up to right now, hon?"

"Thought I'd join you . . . and Sharon."

"I wish you could, but this is business. Maybe we can get together later on, okay?"

Her hand dropped from his shoulder and the lines around her
mouth went taut. "Business, huh?"

"Yeah, Sharon and I have to meet a guy—"

"I'll bet you do."

"Well, that's how it is. I'll call you later."

"Sure. You do that, Willie." She turned and stalked toward the
front of the bar, fringed bag bouncing. One of the urban cowboys
spoke to her, and she tossed her blond mane and snapped at him.
Whatever she said made him slop his beer and turn back to the bar,
shaking his head.

Willie watched her go. "That woman can get madder at me than
anyone I've ever known."

"Some people just have short fuses, I guess."

"Maybe. I don't know, though—sometimes I think it's me. All
my life women have been getting mad at me for practically no
reason, no matter how good I treat them. Sometimes they get violent. My ex-wife tried to bust my head with a quart beer bottle the
day she split." He stared moodily into his glass.

I looked at my watch. Seven-fifteen. "Levin's late."

"So have another beer."

"I think I will." I went and got it, then fell to brooding about
Don and the demo tape. In spite of his living several hours down
the coast, Don and I saw a lot of each other already. What would
happen if he were here in town all the time? Would it be even
better? Or would it spoil things? What if . . . ?

At seven-thirty Willie said, "I don't think Levin's coming."

"Maybe he's having trouble finding the place. He *is* from out of
town, you know."

"Is there any way you can check?"

"No. It was stupid on my part not to at least get a phone number. Wait a minute, though—he did say where he was going. Why don't I check and see if he's been delayed?"

I went to the rear of the bar, where I'd spotted a pay phone, and checked the directory for Rabbi David Halpert. When his phone started to ring, I stuck my finger in my ear to blot out Kenny Rogers's rendition of "The Gambler."

A little girl answered, told me she'd get her daddy, and went away. I listened to a baby crying in the background. Then a strong male voice said, "David Halpert speaking."

I gave my name and explained I was looking for Jerry Levin. "I understand you had an appointment with him late this afternoon."

"With whom?"

"Jerry Levin. He's with the Torah Recovery Committee."

There was a pause. "I'm familiar with the committee, but I don't know Mr. Levin. And I certainly didn't have any appointment today; we just now got back from Marine World."

"You're not the local advisor for the committee's investigator?"

"No, I have no connection with them."

"I see." I thanked him and hung up, then went back to Willie. "It seems Levin's story isn't so straightforward after all. The rabbi he said he was meeting has never heard of him."

"So what now?"

I paused, thinking I should have asked Rabbi Halpert to put me in touch with the committee. "Let's go back to your house. I want to phone the rabbi back, but I don't want to have to talk to him with the jukebox blaring in the background."

Willie nodded, tucked the money pouch inside his denim jacket, and we left the table.

The fog was in now. It crept up the slanting sidestreets, obscuring the facades of the Edwardian row houses and softening the lights on the parking structures of the Medical Center. As we walked up Irving, a streetcar's bell clanged in the mist ahead of us, and then the car came into sight, its wheels wailing on the tracks as it rounded the curve at the top of Arguello. Willie's porchlight beckoned us.

I noticed a piece of paper fluttering on the door. "The note you left for your runners is still there. Aren't you afraid somebody will realize there's no one home and break in?"

"Nope. All the note says is 'Oasis.' I have to do business there pretty often, so one word does it."

"Why do you do business in a bar, anyway?"

"Well, Jesus, you've seen the kind of people I have to deal with. You never know what kind of scum they might be. Until I know a person, I don't just want him calling me or coming to my house. Like I told you before, I got my reputation with the neighbors to consider." He pocketed the note and ushered me inside.

Ahead was a hallway with wine-red carpeting and waist-high wainscoting. A small table lamp provided the only light, and the red-flocked wallpaper above the paneling was oppressive. Willie dropped the leather money pouch on the table. "You want a drink?"

"I don't think so."

"Suit yourself." He started toward the rear of the hall, then paused. "That's funny."

"What is?"

"This door to the garage; I always leave it closed."

"Maybe the wind blew it open."

"No, this is a tight latch." He came back down the hall, then went into the room to my left.

The light he turned on came from a brass chandelier. It revealed more red-flocked wallpaper and dark wainscoting. The room was full of lumpy overstuffed furniture whose cushions had been tossed on the floor. Drawers from two end tables had been pulled out and emptied. Even the box of wood next to the fireplace had been dumped.

Willie whirled and went to the archway at the rear of the room. He flicked on a light above a dining room table. The built-in cabinets there had also been ransacked.

"You're right," he said angrily. "I should be more careful about leaving notes."

I held up a hand for him to be quiet. The only sounds I heard were traffic on the street and the faint murmur of a TV, probably in the house next door. "Let's check upstairs."

"There's nothing up there but my bedroom. I closed off the other rooms after my wife took all the furniture."

"Let's check anyway."

I led him up there cautiously, braced for an attack if the intruder was still in the house. All was quiet. There were four bedrooms, three completely empty. The other had been tossed like the rooms below. I checked the bathroom, but found only a dripping faucet and crumpled towels on the floor.

"How do you suppose he got in?" I said.

"The garage, since the door from there was open. He's probably cleaned me out of my entire stock." Willie started for the stairs.

"I doubt it. From the looks of this, he was after something specific."

"What, though?"

"You would know better than I."

I followed him to the stairs leading to the garage. A light shone somewhere below, toward the rear, where Willie had his office.

"You think he's still down there?" Willie said softly.

"No. We've been making too much noise; it would have scared him off by now." Still, I started down slowly, listening. Willie stayed close behind me.

The piles of cardboard cartons cast elongated shadows on the cement walls. I reached the bottom of the stairs and skirted a stack of old furniture, moving toward the office. A sudden rustling sound came from the front. I stopped, and Willie bumped into me.

"It's the parrot," he said.

"Oh, good Lord." Realizing how silly our sneaking around was, I stepped into the open and went toward the desk. It, too, had been broken into, drawers standing open and chair overturned. The rest of the garage was a shambles.

Clothing had been pulled from racks and dumped on the floor. Cartons had been removed from the shelves and emptied. Toward the front one of the pedestal sinks lay on its side, smashed—and beyond it was a dark form.

Willie came up beside me. I put a hand on his arm.

"What is it?" he said.

I took a deep breath, conscious of the smell for the first time. It was acrid, the way it always is when a gun has been fired in an enclosed space. Acrid, yet sweet, the way it always is when blood has been shed. . . .

Letting go of Willie, I moved forward.

Beyond the smashed sink, Jerry Levin lay on his side. He lay quiet, without breath. His *yarmulke* had fallen off, revealing a bald spot almost the size of the cap. There was a bullet hole in the back of his head.

chapter seven

While the Homicide men and Police Lab personnel took over the garage below, Willie and I sat in his living room amid the disordered furniture. A uniformed cop stood at the door, not exactly guarding us, but giving us little freedom to move or to talk. Not that his presence mattered anyway; Willie sat slumped in a cushionless corner of the couch, arms folded across his chest, silent and withdrawn.

After a few minutes he motioned for me to move over next to him. "I've been trying to figure out if everything's okay down there—my business, you know," he said in a low voice. "So far as I know, it is. It'll be pretty obvious to the cops what all that stuff is, but they won't be able to prove it."

"They'll interrogate you, try to find a connection between your business and Levin."

"I can stand up to it. I have before, without falling apart."

There were voices in the hall near the door to the garage, and the cop went back there. In a few seconds he reappeared, Hank Zahn close behind him. I'd made Willie phone Hank after he'd called the police. In addition to being the fence's lawyer, Hank was mine, and I felt more comfortable having him there.

Hank's eyes, behind his thick horn-rimmed glasses, were filled with concern, but a flicker of amusement crossed his face. "Well, you're a hangdog pair if I ever saw one." He came over and sat down on the coffee table in front of us, his lanky form blocking the cop's view. "What happened?"

Briefly I explained about Levin, our planned meeting with him, and our discovery when we'd returned here. Hank looked around the room, then said to Willie, "You have any idea what he might have been looking for?"

"It's pretty obvious, isn't it? Those Torahs."

Hank nodded, but I said, "Sometimes the obvious can fool you." They both watched me as I got up and went over to one of the end-table drawers that had been dumped on the floor. "Hank, how big is a Torah?"

Hank, who had been bar mitzvahed at thirteen, held up his hands about a yard apart. "Like this."

The drawer was a small one, around a foot square. "Levin

would know a Torah couldn't fit in here. Or in the bedside table drawers that were ransacked upstairs. Or even in that woodbox."

"So what else could he have been looking for?" Hank asked.

"Or *who* else could have been looking? It doesn't have to have been Levin, you know. His killer might—"

Again there were voices in the hall. I turned to the door and stifled a groan when I saw who was standing there.

The Homicide inspector's name was Leo McFate. I knew him slightly because I'd been seeing a lieutenant on that detail when McFate had been transferred from General Works. Earlier tonight I had been afraid my old boyfriend, Greg Marcus, would be the one to be called to the scene—a confrontation that would have been sticky at best. McFate's appearance, however, was ultimately worse.

Between Greg and me there would have been the professional clash between a cop and a private operator, as well as the more basic one between former lovers. With McFate, it would be less a conflict than a complete failure to relate. We just didn't talk, act, or think on the same plane.

Most women would have been delighted at the sight of McFate. He had a tall, muscular body; thick dark brown hair with that distinguished touch of gray at the temples; a luxuriant, well-trimmed mustache; a movie star's cleft chin. He dressed impeccably in designer suits—tonight a three-piece blue pinstripe—and he did all the status things, like going to the symphony and opera and openings at the art museums. Most women would have taken one look at him and seen a real prize.

During our brief acquaintance, however, I'd taken more than one look at Leo McFate. What I saw was a man who worked too hard at getting his name in the gossip columns, a man who did the status things because they were considered "in," not because he enjoyed them. McFate was rumored to be a ladies' man, and his name had been linked with some of the city's most eligible women. But when he talked with the less eligible women—like me—his eyes took on a cool politeness that masked the fact he wasn't really listening. I'd long sensed that, underneath, McFate harbored a deep-seated dislike of women in general and, in fact, was a little afraid of them.

Now he surveyed the room with a faint look of distaste, then nodded to Hank and me. "Counselor. Ms. McCone." His glance flicked to Willie, then back to me. "I presume this is Mr. Whelan, the owner of the house?"

"You got it," Willie muttered. I was somewhat surprised at his surly reaction, but chalked it up to an instant and well-placed dislike of the inspector.

McFate frowned. "Which one of you found the body?"

I said, "I did, I guess."

"You guess?"

"Willie . . . Mr. Whelan and I were together at the time. But I was the first to see it."

"And what time was that?"

"Eight-ten."

"You're certain of that?"

"Yes, I looked at my watch."

"Most women wouldn't have the presence of mind to look at their watches at a time like that."

"I'm not 'most women,'" I said stiffly. "I'm a trained investigator and I try to follow proper procedure. The time was eight-ten."

McFate ran a finger over his handsome mustache. "Very well, Ms. McCone, suppose you tell me how you and Mr. Whelan happened to find the deceased."

I told him, from the beginning, leaving nothing out except the dubious nature of Willie's business. When I finished, McFate was silent for a moment. "You're certain that Rabbi Halpert said he had never heard of Mr. Levin?"

"Yes. He knew of the Torah Recovery Committee, but said he had no connection with them or with Jerry Levin. And after seeing how this house was ransacked, I'm not sure Levin was from the committee at all. He—or someone—was looking for something besides the Torahs—"

McFate held up a hand. "Ms. McCone, let's not jump to conclusions."

"I'm not. You can plainly see—"

"Ms. McCone, please." He turned to Willie. "Mr. Whelan, I understand you told the patrolmen that you're a 'merchandiser' and that the garage is your 'store.'"

"That's right."

"Isn't it true that what you really are is a fence?"

"A what?"

"A fence. A purveyor of stolen goods."

"Purveyor?" Willie looked elaborately blank. "What's . . . Oh, you mean, is that stuff down there stolen?"

"Yes, that's what I mean."

"Hell, no. I bought it all legal. I got receipts, fair and square."

"Yes, Mr. Whelan, I'm sure you do."

"You want to see them?" Willie started to get up.

I glanced at Hank; he was trying not to smile. And much as I disapproved of Willie's line of work, I was fighting back amusement too. It was the opening round between McFate, the stuffy champion of all that was right and proper, and Willie, society's outcast. And I found myself rooting for the underdog.

"That won't be necessary," McFate said.

"No, listen, let me show you."

"Mr. Whelan, all good fences protect themselves with receipts. That doesn't alter the fact that—"

"Now wait a minute!" Willie stood up. Although he was not as muscular, in height he was a match for McFate. "You're saying I'm a fence, and you're also telling me you're not going to give me a chance to prove otherwise?"

"Mr. Whelan—"

"Is that what you're saying?"

"Calm down, please."

Willie turned to Hank. "Isn't that slander or something?"

"Technically."

"Well, make him stop it. You're my lawyer; are you going to stand for that? Tell him we'll sue him."

The corners of Hank's mouth twitched. "McFate, you're baiting my client. I'll have to ask you to stop."

"Mr. Zahn, you're an officer of the court. You can't condone—"

"I'm not condoning anything. I'm merely protecting my client's rights."

"Yeah, I got rights the same as anybody else."

McFate gave an exasperated sigh. Willie stood there, quivering with manufactured indignation. I made the mistake of looking at Hank, and then involuntarily started to laugh. I tried to force it down, but that only made it well up faster. I swallowed, and what came out was a snort.

Willie turned and stared at me. Hank rolled his eyes at the ceiling. McFate's mouth turned down in disgust.

I clapped my hand over my mouth and snorted again.

"For God's sake, Sharon," Hank said.

"Oh, Lord, I'm sorry, I can't—" I doubled over laughing, arms clutched around my midsection.

"You all right?" Willie asked.

I snorted again.

"Sharon, stop it." Hank's voice was stern.

"I'm trying."

"Good."

I remained doubled over, breathing deeply to get myself under control. When I looked up, McFate's imperturbable expression was once more in place. "Would you like a glass of water, Ms. McCone?" he asked coldly.

"No, I'm all right now."

"Then perhaps you'd like to be excused. You can give us a formal statement tomorrow."

"But—"

"That will be all for now."

"But what about—"

"Sharon," Hank said, "I think the inspector is done questioning you." He jerked his head toward the door.

I got up, feeling a little weak. "Okay, I'll see you back at the office."

"Yes. I want to talk to you."

"Wait a minute," Willie said to me. "Can you do me a favor?"

"Sure."

"Will you stop by Alida's place and explain why I can't call her? She lives over on Ninth Avenue, seventeen-twenty-seven, bottom apartment."

"I'll be glad to." As I turned to leave the room, I bumped into McFate and stepped on his polished black shoe. He moved back, glowering at me, and extended one hand toward the door. I fled.

chapter eight

Alida Edwards's building was five blocks from Golden Gate Park, where the avenues began to slope upward into the middle-class neighborhood known as Sunset Heights. Diagonally across the street from it was a white structure that looked like a community center; a sign announced it was the headquarters of the Sunset Heights Association of Responsible People. Briefly I wondered who these people were and what they were responsible for that warranted a clubhouse. Of one thing I was certain: Had I lived in this neighborhood, I would not have been asked to join.

I pressed Alida's bell, received an answering buzz, and crossed a tiled lobby to the door to the downstairs apartment. The blond-haired woman looked out, raising her eyebrows when she saw me.

"Willie asked me to stop by," I said. "He won't be able to call you as he promised, and he wanted me to explain."

The lines around her mouth tightened. "Got some hot deal going, huh?"

"Not exactly."

"What then?"

"I don't think you want me to go into it in the lobby, where your neighbors can hear."

Ungraciously she flung the door open and stalked off down a long hallway.

I closed the door behind me and followed her into a large room that was sparsely furnished with an open, rumpled hide-a-bed and a Danish modern dining table. Its walls were hung with Indian weavings, and earth-toned pottery sat on some shelves near the tiny kitchen. A large window overlooked a floodlit backyard land-scaped with fig trees and fuchsias.

I was about to tell her how attractive I found her place when a woman's voice called to her from the next room. It sounded famil-iar, so I followed Alida in there. The room was outfitted with a worktable and cabinets, and in its center stood Selena Gonzalez. She was admiring an intricate gold band that coiled around her arm.

"Alida, I will take this one," she said. "The snake bracelet with eyes of agate." Then she saw me and grinned. "So, we meet again."

"You know each other?" Alida asked.

"We met earlier today at the flea market," I said.

"Of course. In addition to being a fellow vendor, Selena's my next-door neighbor—and one of my best customers." Abruptly Alida had shifted into amiability. I wondered if all her mood swings were this sudden.

While Selena paid for the bracelet, I went over to a display cabinet that contained jewelry on black velvet pads. Made of gold and polished bits of stone, most of the pieces incorporated animal shapes. I didn't particularly like them, but one medallion of a lion with gleaming blue eyes wasn't too bad.

We went back to the larger room, and Alida began straightening the covers on the bed. Selena and I sat crosslegged on the floor, the Mexican woman still admiring the bracelet. Alida quickly gave up on the rumpled bed and flopped in its center, hugging a pillow.

"So what's Willie's excuse tonight?" she said.

"It's no excuse. There was a murder at his house. The police are questioning him about it."

Alida sat up straighter. Selena looked up from the bracelet. There was a heavy silence. Then Alida asked, "Who was killed?"

"The man we were supposed to meet at the Oasis. He was shot in Willie's garage."

"When?"

"Sometime while we were in the bar, I assume."

"Who was he?"

Odd, I thought, that she didn't bother to ask if Willie was all right. "The man who had been watching Willie's stall at the flea market.

Selena sucked in her breath. She was very pale. "The evil one with the little eyes."

"What was he doing in Willie's garage?" Alida asked.

"I don't know."

"How'd he get in there?"

"I don't know that either."

There was another silence. Then Selena said, "Evil begets evil."

Alida flashed her an irritated glance. "We can do without your Latin American philosophy, thank you." To me she said, "What was the dead guy's name?"

"Jerry Levin."

"And you say he was shot?"

"Yes."

"With what kind of gun?"

"Again, I don't know. I didn't see a gun near the body." I wondered if the police had found the weapon. McFate hadn't said.

"God," Alida said. "That's what they get for not passing the gun control ordinance. If people weren't free to walk around with the things—"

"Nonsense." Selena shook her head. "It is the outlaws who use them to kill. Outlaws always know how to get guns."

"That's an overworked and illogical argument." Alida turned to me. "Isn't that so?"

"Yes."

"You're a detective. Do you carry—"

Selena interrupted her. "A what?" she asked.

"A detective," Alida said.

The Mexican woman put a hand to her throat. "Police . . . ?"

I realized why she was so anxious. "No, private."

"Willie hired her to find out about the man who was killed," Alida added.

"Oh." Selena fell silent, her finger tracing the coils of her new bracelet.

"Do you carry a gun?" Alida asked me. It was what she'd started to ask before.

"Very seldom. I own two, and I know how to use them. But no, I don't carry one unless I'm going into a very dangerous situation."

"You're like me," she said. "My daddy taught me to shoot straight when I was just a kid—they do things that way in Texas. But I wouldn't have a gun in the house. Unlike some people." She cast a baleful glance at Selena.

"I live alone over there in a ground-floor apartment." Selena jerked a thumb at the wall behind her. "I feel unsafe, so I have a gun that I bought from Fat Herman."

"Fat Herman?" I asked.

"The man who sells the knives at the flea market."

"The one who wears the beach-umbrella hat."

"Yes. He has a gun shop on Mission Street. He was kind enough to advise—"

"Did he also advise you that your gun is likely to be taken away from you and used against you?" Alida said.

Selena frowned. "Let us not argue." She turned to me. "Have you ever shot anyone?"

"Yes."

"What was it like?"

"Very unpleasant."

"Did the person die?"

"Yes." I got up to go.

"Who was it you shot?" Selena asked.

"Christ, don't you see she doesn't want to talk about it?"

"Was it, as they say, in the line of duty?"

"Selena . . ."

I sighed. "It was in connection with a case, yes. He was a murderer, and he was trying to kill one of my friends. It's nothing I'm proud of. It was just something I had to do." Then I went down the hall to the front door.

Alida followed me. "I love Selena dearly, but she doesn't know when to stop."

"That's okay. Probably I should just have said no when she first asked about it."

Alida paused, her hand on the doorknob. "Look, do you think the cops will arrest Willie?"

"Why should they?"

"Well, the guy *was* killed in his house. And cops don't really take to Willie."

"You mean, because he's a fence?"

Alida's mouth went tight and prim. "Willie's a businessman. But sometimes the way he does business looks funny."

How could she believe that? I wondered. But if she wanted to fool herself it was all right with me. "His lawyer's there with him. I think the cops will give him a rough time, but they don't have anything to hold him on."

She nodded, looking relieved.

I went outside and walked up the street past the responsible people's clubhouse to my car. It was time to go to All Souls and see if Hank had returned. As I put my key in the ignition, however, a sudden thought came to me.

Selena Gonzalez was an illegal alien. Under state law, no weapons dealer could sell a gun to her. No reputable dealer would. That made Fat Herman as much on the far side of the law as Willie.

The office windows of All Souls's big brown Victorian were lit up, in spite of it being after eleven o'clock. As I went down the central hall, I could hear several men yelling at the tops of their lungs in the law library. I stopped to listen, but couldn't make out the words.

Anne Marie Altman, a stunning blond tax lawyer whose demeanor was as calm and restrained as her legal specialty, emerged from the kitchen. She wore a terrycloth bathrobe and was munching on a piece of toast.

"What's happening in there?" I asked. "Who's about to kill whom?"

She grinned and licked peanut butter off one finger. "Oh, that's just Harold and that idiot client of his who's running for supervisor. And the client's campaign manager and a couple of aides, I guess."

"But what're they yelling about?"

"Didn't you see today's paper?"

"Not all of it."

Her eyes sparkled. "Well, apparently our candidate didn't either—not until about an hour ago. And now he's in quite a state. It seems that that investigative reporter—J. D. Smith—did an exposé of his indiscretions while serving on the Planning Commission. Pretty juicy stuff. Our candidate came over here with the idea of suing, but from what I've heard, he's now in favor of tearing J. D. Smith apart, limb from limb. The others are trying to persuade him it's not a good idea. I, personally, think a straitjacket is in order."

"Not bad for a Sunday night, huh?"

"No." Momentarily Anne Marie looked mournful. "I wanted to watch an old movie on the TV in the living room—*Godzilla Versus King Kong*. But I can't hear a thing over that ruckus. Guess I'll go upstairs and catch up on my reading." She wandered off toward the stairway to the second floor, where several of the attorneys lived in free rooms that were partial compensation for the co-op's dismally low salaries.

I went to Hank's office and looked in. The lights were off; the stacks of newspapers, magazines, and miscellaneous periodicals that my boss stockpiled hulked in the darkness. McFate must still be questioning Willie.

Rather than go to the converted closet that was my office, I sat down behind Hank's desk and pulled an old issue of *National Geographic* off one of the stacks. I was partway through an article on coyotes when Hank arrived.

He motioned for me to keep his chair, then slumped in the one reserved for clients. His face was weary and he ran his hand through his tight curls like a cranky child. The shouting was still going on down the hall, but he didn't appear to notice.

"What happened with Willie?" I asked.

"They booked him on suspicion."

"But why? We were together at the Oasis when Levin was shot. A lot of people saw us—"

"You're making a false assumption. According to the medical

examiner, Levin was killed no later than five-thirty, long before you and Willie met at the bar."

"Well, doesn't he have an alibi for that time?"

"No. Or if he does, he won't say. He claims he was riding around alone in his truck."

"And you don't believe that?"

Hank shrugged.

"Why not?"

"Something about the way he said it. I suspect he may have been doing something illegal at the time. That's the trouble with having a client in Willie's line of work."

We were silent for a moment. At least, I thought, this turn of events had driven my disgraceful behavior with McFate from Hank's mind. "Hank," I finally said, "why do you represent Willie anyway?"

"He's a friend, an old friend. And, anyway, I owe him something."

"What?"

"My life."

"You mean, in Vietnam—"

"Yes. Look, Shar, I don't really want to talk about it now."

"So that's why you didn't warn me he was a fence when you sent me to see him. You wanted me to take the job, but you knew I'd have reservations. So you sent me to the flea market, hoping my curiosity and Willie's charm would do the trick."

"It worked, didn't it? Let's just say I owe Willie a debt that will never be repaid. And because of that I'll continue to represent him, even if he did actually kill Levin."

"You can't believe he did it."

"It's late, and I'm tired, and I don't know what to believe."

"Do you want me to stay on the case?"

"Yes. If they can make this charge stick, I'm going to have to build a defense, and I'm afraid, from his behavior tonight, that I won't get much help from Willie."

"Okay. Tell me one thing: Did the police find the weapon?"

"Yes. It was to one side of Levin's body, under some shelves."

"What kind of gun was it?"

"A twenty-two. When McFate showed it to Willie, he commented that it was the 'classic Saturday Night Special.'"

That, I thought, would probably mean it was an RG-14, a gun assembled of imported parts by R.G. Industries, a Florida firm.

The parts do not meet the U.S. specifications for size and metal, and the gun costs under a hundred dollars—a fact that greatly adds to its appeal. "What was Willie's reaction to the gun?"

Hank shifted uncomfortably in his chair. "He seemed surprised."

"You mean, he may have recognized it?"

"I thought so."

"Was there anything distinctive about it?"

"A triangular chip out of the grip. McFate also commented on that."

"All right." I stood up. "In the morning I'll start with a man who sells weapons at the flea market. He might be able to tell me if Willie is the owner of that twenty-two."

"The police will check that out with state firearms registration."

"I doubt they'll learn anything. Even knowing Willie for as short a time as I have, I'm fairly certain he wouldn't bother to buy a weapon legally. And, if it's the kind of gun I think it is, it's a type that is commonly traded under the counter."

"And this weapons dealer is the one Willie would have gone to?"

"Probably."

Hank took off his glasses and began polishing them on the hem of his trenchcoat. His head drooped dispiritedly. He always took his clients' problems to heart—often too much to heart—and Willie's would upset him even more than usual.

"Also," I went on, "I'll talk to Rabbi Halpert and see if I can't get him to put me in touch with the Torah Recovery Committee. We need to know more about Jerry Levin."

"Okay. I'll expect you to check in with me tomorrow afternoon."

I looked at my watch. "*This* afternoon; it's past midnight." Past midnight, and Don would be wondering what had happened to me.

I stepped out into the hall. The yelling in the law library had stopped. When I said good night to Hank, he was holding his glasses, staring at their polished lenses.

chapter nine

The next morning I went down to the Hall of Justice and gave a formal statement. McFate was mercifully absent, and the inspector I talked to, a man called Gallagher whose first name I could never remember, was someone I'd known and liked for years. When I'd first met him, Gallagher had been an earnest and idealistic young man who admired me extravagantly. He still admired me, but every time I saw him he looked less earnest and idealistic and more and more tired. When I was done at the Hall, I looked up the address of Herman's Gun Shop in the phone book and drove over there.

The shop was on a seedy block on Mission not far from the Twenty-fourth Street BART station. About ten years ago an attempt had been made at beautifying upper Mission; the city had planted trees and laid ceramic tiles in bright colors that were supposed to embody the area's Spanish character. But the palm trees had died and the tiles were now cracked and dirty. If anything, the district had slid deeper into poverty and hopelessness.

When I entered the small store, two youthful urban cowboys who might have been enlisted men on leave were standing in front of a case that housed a .44 Magnum.

"Quite a weapon," one said, nodding approvingly.

"Could tear a hell of a hole in someone," the other agreed.

I shuddered and kept going toward the back of the store, where the cash register was. A fat man with grizzled hair sat there, a genial smile on his fleshy face. Without his beach-umbrella hat, I almost didn't recognize Fat Herman.

He recognized me, though, because the smile grew wider, exposing gapped teeth. "Hey, you're Willie Whelan's new runner. Somebody pointed you out to me at the market yesterday."

"Yes, I am." I'd debated what approach to use with Fat Herman in the small hours of the morning while I stared at the bedroom ceiling and Don slept the sleep of the just beside me. He'd barely woken when I'd crawled into bed, except to mumble something unintelligible to me, and I hadn't known whether to feel relieved or insulted. But his deep sleep and my wakefulness had given me plenty of time to plot strategy, and in the end I'd decided it was best to maintain my role as Willie's runner. That was made all the more possible by the fact that, while the morning newspaper account of Levin's slaying had mentioned my name, it had neglected to give my occupation. Or, more likely, McFate had neglected to mention it. I had a hunch the inspector didn't approve of women being private investigators; in his mind, therefore, I wasn't one.

Herman said, "That was some trouble at Willie's place last night, huh?"

"I guess you saw the paper."

"First thing. Did they really arrest him?"

"Yes."

"But he didn't do it."

"No." I only wished Hank had Fat Herman's confidence in Willie. Or mine, for that matter. I didn't know why, but a gut-level instinct told me the fence hadn't killed Levin.

"Fucking cops." Herman glanced at the two young men, whose heads turned. They frowned in disapproval. The gun dealer glared at them, and they looked away. "So what can I do for you? Willie send you?"

"No, I came because . . . well, after what happened last night, I'm afraid. I live alone in a ground-floor flat, and I've decided I need a gun for protection. Selena Gonzalez told me you had helped her choose one, and I hoped you might be able to help me too."

"Sure. What I sold Selena is a High Standard Sentinel Deluxe. Twenty-two caliber nine-shot. You know anything about guns?"

"No," I lied.

"Well, it's not much of a weapon. Just a plinker, good for shooting at tin cans. But Selena's a little bitty woman. She talks big, but she's never going to pull that gun on anybody. So I let her have it for a hundred and a quarter and she feels safe."

Herman stood up and surveyed me, his little eyes moving up and down my body in a way that made me feel crawly. "Now, you're a substantial lady. You could handle more of a gun, if you're serious about protecting yourself."

"I am."

"I got an older gun you might be interested in." Again Herman glanced at the young men, who were now examining a case full of rifles. "British, Smith and Wesson, World War Two service revolver. Military people like it for self-defense."

And, I thought, dealers like you favor it because usually a gun that old can't be traced. "How much would it run?"

"For a friend of Willie's, a hundred and a half."

"That's a lot of money."

"This gun is practically a collector's item. You decide you don't want it around, you can sell it at a tidy profit. Or I'd take it back, refund most of your money."

And resell it at that tidy profit, I thought. "I see." I paused. "What about the waiting period?"

"The what?"

"I heard there's a fifteen-day waiting period, so the cops can check the buyer's record. I wouldn't want to wait—I'm scared *now*."

Herman grinned broadly. "For a friend of Willie's? You want the gun, you take it home with you."

"Can I see it?"

"Sure, but first I better take care of these customers." Herman lumbered around the counter, his paunch hanging over the belt of his khaki pants. "You fellas want anything?" he asked the two young men.

They looked at each other and shrugged.

"'Cause if you don't," Herman went on, "you'd better be moving on. This is a gun shop, not a museum."

They made grumbling noises, but headed for the door.

"Soldiers. You can tell them a mile away, even now that the military's relaxed the regs about hair." Herman went back around the counter and through a curtained archway. "Soldiers," his voice went on, "they never have any money, but they're always looking." He returned in a moment and placed a gun in my hands.

It was snub-nosed, with a top break—a gun that would do a lot of damage at close range. I turned it over, handling it awkwardly, as if I had never touched one before.

"What do you think?" Herman said.

"It's . . . ugly, isn't it?" I didn't have to fake my distaste. I'm good with guns, a crack shot on the range. I take a certain pleasure in target practice, the way I would in any professional skill. But I took no pleasure in handling this .38. It's true that all guns are made to kill, but to a person who's familiar with them, some guns are more deadly than others.

"Depends on your point of view, I guess," Herman said. "To me, what you've got there is a precision instrument. An instrument of survival."

I set the gun on the counter. "I suppose you sell to a lot of the flea market people—like Willie?"

"Willie?" Herman chuckled. "You wouldn't catch Willie with a piece. Between him and that blond broad of his—what's her name?"

"Alida."

"Yeah, Alida. Between the two of them, you've got an anti-gun lobby that would beat out the NRA if they ever got organized."

"I didn't realize that."

"No? Well, from what I hear, Willie got turned off by guns in Vietnam. He doesn't say much about it, but I bet if you could get it out of him, he'd have a hell of a story why. Vietnam worked that way—or the opposite. Guys either came home loving guns or hating them." He paused, shaking his head. "Yeah, they love them or they hate them."

"What about the other folks at the markets? Willie's runners, for instance—did any of them ever buy from you?"

His little eyes narrowed. "Why do you ask?"

"Well, what if Willie found out I owned a gun? Would he disapprove enough to fire me? I need the job and I'd sure hate to lose it—"

This time Herman laughed loudly. "I wouldn't worry."

"Why not?"

"If Willie was that intolerant, he'd never be able to make it on the flea market scene."

"What do you mean?"

"Well, look at those people—they're all rednecks. I sell more guns out at the market than anything else."

"But all I saw at your stand was knives."

"I don't display the guns for all the world to see, little girl. But folks know to ask for them anyway."

I touched the .38 thoughtfully with my index finger. "And the cops don't bother you?"

"Hell, no. Marchetti sees to that."

"Mack Marchetti knows you're selling guns out there?"

"Sure. And turns his back—for a price."

"A price?" I feigned innocence.

Herman leaned on the counter, his hands spread flat. "I can tell you're new on the scene. You don't think Marchetti makes his money by renting out spaces for seven bucks a day, do you?"

"I don't know. I hadn't thought about it."

"Well, think. If you had hold of a piece of land where every kind of illegal activity in the book was going on, what would you do?"

"Take a cut of it, I guess."

"You guess." Herman snorted. "Little girl, you're not going to do too well in the business if all you can do is guess at it."

"Okay, now that you've mentioned it, it makes sense. Mack Marchetti takes a cut, in exchange for letting you people operate."

"Right. And then what does Marchetti do with part of that cut?"

"He pays off the cops, I suppose."

"Does that surprise you, little girl—that there are crooked cops?"

"No."

"Good. Now maybe you're on your way to being of some use to Willie."

Maybe I am, I thought, but not in the way you imagine.

"So do you want this gun?" Herman asked.

"I'm going to have to think about it. It's a lot of money."

"What's money, compared to your life?"

"You have a point."

"You bet I do. Tell you what—you think about it. The gun'll be here for a while. But don't wait too long."

"I won't."

I started for the door, glancing at the cases on either side of me as I went. The guns lay there, gleaming black and sleek and deadly.

chapter ten

"I hope you'll excuse the mess." David Halpert looked dismayed at the chaos in his living room—not so much for my sake, but because it was his and he had to live with it.

The rabbi's house was a small Victorian in Bernal Heights, on the other side of the hill from All Souls. The living room walls had been stripped for replastering, and the furniture was heaped in the center and covered with dusty plastic drop cloths. Tools and buckets of joint compound stood by the bay window, and two rolled rugs blocked the doorway to the hall. In the middle of all this sat a baby in diapers; it was chewing on a new paint roller.

"That's okay." I looked around for a place to sit. The only available piece of furniture was an uncomfortable-looking park bench. "I'm renovating my house, too."

"Really?" Halpert's eyes gleamed eagerly behind wire-rimmed glasses. It was a response I'd gotten used to receiving from other owners of partly restored houses. "How long have you been working on it?" he asked.

"About three months. I'm almost done with my living room."

"Oh." His face fell and he looked around, shoulders slumping inside his "Save the Whales" T-shirt. "We've lived here four years. This room has been like this for six months. There's never any time. . . ."

"I shouldn't wonder, with all your other activities."

"Yes, plus my wife travels a lot on account of her job, and then there are the two kids."

As if on cue, the baby started to cry. Halpert scooped it up and cradled it expertly against his shoulder. The cries stopped. I smiled at the contrast between the infant and the big bear of a man. In cutoff jeans and no shoes, his black hair curling wildly around his head, David Halpert fit my image of a crusading young rabbi.

The baby began to beat on Halpert's head with the paint roller. He caught its hand and said, "I'd better put her in her playpen. Normally I don't believe in incarcerating children, but then again . . . Excuse me a minute." He stepped over the rolled rugs and went down the hallway toward the rear of the house.

Resigned to discomfort, I sat down on the park bench. It was close to noon, and last night's fog had burned off early; the temperature had risen to un-San Francisco-like heights. I took off my light jacket and folded it on the bench beside me. Halpert returned in a moment, dragging a kitchen chair behind him, and threw open the front window.

"It's been a hectic morning," he said, seating himself on the chair. "Did I mention that the police were here?"

"No. They got to you fast."

"Oh, yes—it was no later than ten o'clock. They showed me a picture of the dead man." His dark eyes grew troubled. "I recognized him. I should have recognized his name when you called last night. But it had been several years and, frankly, it was one of those unpleasant experiences you try to forget."

"Could you start at the beginning? Where did you know Jerry Levin?"

"Here in San Francisco. Do you remember about five years ago when the Hillel Foundation at San Francisco State was fire-bombed?"

Hillel was the Jewish student organization. "Yes. The police thought it was the work of a neo-Nazi group, but they couldn't prove it."

"Jerry Levin was one of the men they arrested and later let go."

"But—"

"But he was Jewish. Yes."

"Why would he join such a group?"

"Alienation. It's a key word of our times."

"Alienation from his religion, you mean?"

"And his people. Our customs, our history, our very life-style, if you want to call it that."

"I can see why someone might stop going to church . . . temple, I mean. I'm a lapsed Catholic myself. But I've never felt the need to firebomb the Newman Center."

Halpert looked uncomfortable. "Catholicism, perhaps, is not so pervasive a tradition as Judaism. Our customs, if strictly followed, can be very constraining. And then, of course, there's the history of persecution, which can induce a certain paranoia . . ."

Halpert was obviously one of the new breed who can be found in all branches of organized religion: modern thinkers who like to mix their age-old beliefs with a good dose of psychology. It was a school of thought I didn't much understand, having been raised in the God-will-get-you-if-you're-not-good brand of Catholicism.

I said, "Did you actually know Jerry Levin?"

"I met him in jail, after the firebombing."

"*You* were in jail?"

"No, not that time." Halpert made an impatient gesture. "I went to see Levin. I was affiliated with Hillel then and I thought I might be able to help the man. Or if not help him, at least gain some understanding of why he had done such a thing."

"You're certain he did?"

"I wasn't until I talked with him. Actually, talked isn't quite the word. It was an unpleasant scene, with him raging and screaming at me. It convinced me of his involvement in the firebombing."

I tried to reconcile his picture of Levin with the timid, inept young man I'd talked with the day before, but couldn't. "Was Levin a student at State?"

"Yes, in the drama department. Apparently he was an excellent actor; his instructors thought he had quite a future on the stage. But after the police released him, he dropped out of school and vanished."

Now it made more sense. Levin had been employing his acting skills when he'd told me the story of the Torah Recovery Committee. But to what end? "Were you able to contact any members of the committee, by the way?" I asked. Halpert had promised to do so when we'd set this appointment early in the morning.

"Yes." He looked at his watch. "In fact, Ben Cohen, their Bay Area representative, is due here about now. He knows of Levin too, and I thought you'd like to hear what he has to say firsthand." He stood up. "Shall I make some coffee?"

"Don't go to any trouble on my account."

"It's no trouble. Besides, I think I'd better. Ben has never been to the house before, and he's going to be shocked at this mess. Maybe coffee will take his mind off it."

While Halpert fixed the coffee, I wandered around the living room, stretching out the kinks that the hard bench had put in my back. The rabbi returned with a tray, and I held it while he dragged a scarred end table out from under the drop cloth. He arranged the ceramic coffeepot, matching cups, and silver spoons on the table, then went back for cream, sugar, and cloth napkins. I frowned, wondering if the attractive display didn't just call attention to its disordered surroundings. When the doorbell rang, Halpert was there with all the efficiency of a butler.

Ben Cohen was a stocky man with gray hair and a matching pale gray suit. Halpert introduced us and unobtrusively dusted off the kitchen chair before offering it to his guest. The two of us sat on the bench and Halpert served coffee. After a glance at the room, Cohen devoted himself to adding sugar and stirring. He sipped his coffee and nodded appreciatively, then spoke in a deep, slow voice.

"Miss McCone, I understand you have been investigating this man, Levin."

"Yes. I work for the attorney of the man who has been accused of Jerry Levin's murder. I'm trying to build our defense."

"Then perhaps, as David has suggested, I should tell you what we—the Torah Recovery Committee—know of Mr. Levin. Anything you can add to that, of course, will help us."

"Help you with what?"

"The recovery of the scrolls that are still missing. But I'll get to that shortly. You know what our work is?"

"Yes."

He paused, stirring his coffee, obviously taking the time to gather his thoughts. "The first time we—our private investigators—became aware of Mr. Levin was well over two years ago. A young man of his description had appeared at the Temple Beth Israel in White Plains, New York, claiming to be a journalist doing an article on congregations in the New York area. He was very convincing, and the rabbi gave him permission to talk to members of the congregation. For several weeks thereafter, the man literally had the run of the synagogue. Then, suddenly, he disappeared, and at the same time, so did the temple's Torahs."

"Were the police called in?"

"Yes, but it was too late. The Torahs were gone, and the man had vanished completely. There was not really any proof he had taken the scrolls. But no one at the magazine he mentioned had ever been approached about such an article, nor had they ever heard the name he used.

"If this had been an isolated incident, our interest probably would have stopped there. But soon after that, events repeated themselves. First at a temple in Yonkers, and again in Elizabeth, New Jersey. All in all, Mr. Levin robbed thirteen temples in New York, New Jersey, and Pennsylvania over a two-year period."

"But how could he do that? Surely the thefts received publicity. Wouldn't the congregations have been alert to someone of Levin's description who claimed to be a journalist?"

"Levin didn't always claim to be a member of the press. At one temple, he posed as a Ph.D. candidate doing a thesis. At another, he took pictures, saying he was a photographer putting together a book. There was endless variety to his stories. And—according to the congregations—he was also extremely convincing."

"Yes, I imagine so. He certainly did a job of that on me yesterday, when he claimed to be an investigator for your committee. But how did you learn his real identity?"

"Purely by coincidence. The last synagogue the ingratiating young man approached was Temple Emanu-el, in King of Prussia, Pennsylvania, near Philadelphia. There he was once again posing as a magazine writer; probably he assumed he was far enough away from White Plains that he could resume his first disguise. And using the same story as he had earlier was not what gave him away."

"What did, then?" Halpert asked.

"A member of the congregation—a man who had recently

moved east from San Francisco—recognized him as one of the men who had been arrested for the firebombing of the Hillel Foundation here. He went to the rabbi, but before they could confront Levin about it, he, and three of the temple's Torahs, disappeared. It was unfortunate he got away, but at least we could identify him."

"So you hired investigators in San Francisco," I said.

"Yes. They showed Levin's picture to various congregations, both here and in other parts of the state, who had unwittingly purchased stolen Torahs during the past two years. They all identified Levin as the seller. Again, he had appeared so charming and sincere that no one had thought to question the rightful ownership of the scrolls he was selling until it was too late."

"Didn't that pretty much put him out of business?"

"It did. We've sent his picture and explanatory material to every congregation in the United States. But we are still interested in Mr. Levin's recent activities because a number of the Torahs he stole— seven, to be exact—are still missing. We have had him under surveillance a great deal of the time since we learned who he was and our investigators located him here. But he had not led us to those Torahs—and now he never will."

I swirled the dregs of my coffee around in my cup, thinking over my conversation with Levin. Cohen watched me expectantly. Finally I said, "I don't think Levin had possession of the scrolls when he died."

"Why not?"

"Because he claimed to be looking for them. A lot of what he told me was lies, but I think they were designed to make his activities more plausible. Somehow those scrolls had gotten out of his hands, and he wanted them back."

Cohen nodded and poured him more coffee. This time he didn't bother to add sugar.

I said, "What did your investigators find out about Jerry Levin? What had he been doing in the time between the firebombing and his appearance on the East Coast?"

"Initially he was living in a cabin in the Santa Cruz Mountains. There's not too much information on his activities during that period; he seemed to have been fairly reclusive. After he started robbing the synagogues, he maintained the cabin and was in and out of there from time to time."

"Probably when he came west to unload some of the Torahs."

"Yes. A month after he was recognized in King of Prussia, he made a final attempt to sell a Torah to a Palo Alto synagogue. The rabbi recognized him from the picture our investigators had shown him, and excused himself to call the police. Apparently Levin sensed the danger, because he was gone, along with the Torah, when the rabbi returned to the room."

"And this was when?"

"Three months ago. Our investigators later learned he had remained in the cabin for one of those months, but then it burned to the ground. Soon afterward he turned up here in San Francisco, in a Tenderloin hotel. After that—until last night—he frequented the flea market on the frontage road near Brisbane, as well as the vicinity of Mr. Whelan's house."

"Were your investigators following him last night?"

Cohen shook his head ruefully. "No. We'd had to cut back our surveillance; unfortunately, our funds are not limitless."

For a moment, the only sound in the room was a fly buzzing against the upper panel of the bay window. Then I said, "This cabin in the Santa Cruz Mountains—can you tell me how to get there?"

Cohen looked surprised. "Yes, I've visited the site. It's near Boulder Creek." He took out a pencil and a small notebook and drew a map that seemed reasonably in scale. "Why, may I ask, do you want to go there? It's nothing now but charred wood."

"I don't know that I do. But I need to know much more about Levin if I'm to build a defense for Willie Whelan."

"Won't the police check out Levin's background, including that cabin?"

"The police have a plausible subject. They'll concentrate on that end, building a case that will stand up in court."

Cohen nodded. "Have you anything to add to what you've already told me?"

"No, I don't. I only spoke to Levin the one time, and then I found him dead."

"Then I had better be on my way." He stood and handed me a card. "That's where you can reach me." With a last interested glance around the room, he started for the door, Halpert following.

"Mr. Cohen," I said.

He turned as he was about to step over the rolled rugs.

"May I ask you something?"

"Certainly."

"Why didn't your committee simply turn the matter of Levin and the stolen Torahs over to the police?"

"We intended to, once we had recovered the Torahs."

"You didn't think the police would recover them for you?"

"Perhaps. But their main concern would have been apprehending Levin. Ours was ensuring that the Torahs survived." He smiled then, a smile that contrasted sharply to his wintry eyes. "Besides, Miss McCone, our people are accustomed to doing things for themselves."

As I watched David Halpert show Cohen out, I remembered the men and women who had devoted their lives to hunting down Nazi war criminals. Yes, I thought. His people certainly were accustomed to doing things for themselves. And with good cause.

chapter eleven

I stopped at a *tacquería* on Mission Street and bought a beef burrito, then went back to All Souls. As I came through the front door, our secretary, Ted, stared at the bag I was carrying and said, "Uh-oh." Most of the folks at the co-op were food faddists—I think that year it was *sushi*—and their tolerance for Mexican fast food was limited.

Hank was the only person in the kitchen, however, so nobody was going to pick on me about my poor dietary habits today. Like me, my boss would eat anything. He was always whipping up pots of hearty chili or exotic curries, at which the others turned up their noses. It was funny, though, how those leftovers mysteriously disappeared in the dead of night.

I unwrapped my burrito, got a Coke, and joined him at the big oak table. He was polishing off a Dagwood sandwich and reading a rough draft of a brief. One of the pages had a big mustard smudge on it.

"What's happening with Willie?" I said.

"The arraignment's at two o'clock. I've already talked with the judge and the D.A.'s man. Willie should be out on bail by tonight."

Bail in capital-offense cases was usually high. "Can he afford it?"

"Don't let Willie's appearance or lifestyle fool you; he's managed to sock away plenty of cash in his day. How are things coming on your end?"

I told him about my talks with Fat Herman, David Halpert, and Ben Cohen. Noncommittally silent, he continued eating.

"Hank," I said, "this would be much simpler if you could persuade Willie to tell you where he was when Levin was killed. You're his friend; can't you just lay it on the line for him?"

"I intend to."

"Good. Will you also tell him to do something for me?"

"What?"

"Search his house from top to bottom for those Torahs."

"Didn't someone already do that?"

"Not necessarily. Even if that was what he was after, we don't know that he found them. That's a big house, and there's a lot of junk in it."

"You really think the Torahs are there?"

"Levin seemed to think so, and he invested a lot of time in watching Willie."

"All right, I'll tell him to look." Hank stood up and took his empty plate to the dishwasher. "In the meantime, where will you be?"

"In the Santa Cruz Mountains, researching Jerry Levin's past." I tossed the Coke can and the foil the burrito had come in into the trash, then went to my office and called home. It had occurred to me that Don might enjoy an excursion in the hills. The phone was picked up by my answering service, and I remembered then that Don had said something about delivering his demo tape and taking a tour of the KSUN studios today.

That was just as well, I decided as I hung up. I was preoccupied with the problem of Willie Whelan and probably wouldn't be very good company. Besides, I could accomplish the trip in far less time alone. I gassed up the MG at my usual station, then headed south on Interstate 280.

Following Ben Cohen's hand-drawn map, I left Highway 17 at Old Summit Road south of Los Gatos. The road curved up into the mountains; it was in reasonably good repair and lined with expensive homes on thickly landscaped lots. Then, after about five miles, it narrowed and the pavement deteriorated somewhat. I came to a couple of forks that weren't indicated on Cohen's map and followed the branches that looked most promising. Houses were no longer in evidence, save for a few mailboxes, and the road continued to climb, winding in switchbacks through rocky terrain that was covered with scrub oak, pepper trees, and occasional scraggly pines.

Finally the road became a mere cut in the hillside, walled on one side by dirt and rock to which ferns clung. On the other, it dropped off sharply. At a wide spot I pulled off and got out of the car. From there I could look over the tops of trees to the soft contours of the mountains on the distant horizon. Although it was a sunny day, a light haze made them bluish-green. Across the valley a vineyard clung to a hillside. Somewhere in the underbrush below a stream trickled, and a jay scolded me from a nearby branch.

I looked at Cohen's map again. There was no telling if I'd followed the right forks or come far enough. I debated going back, but decided this road probably came out at Boulder Creek. If I arrived there without finding Levin's place, I would ask directions.

After a few more miles, however, I suddenly came upon the barbed-wire fence and rusty wagon wheel that the map indicated as marking Levin's property. The driveway consisted of two ruts that snaked off down the hill from the road. I considered whether the MG's suspension could withstand the bumps, and decided to leave the car where it was. The overgrown tracks descended steeply for some distance and then bottomed out at a plank bridge that crossed the little creek. The water, running swiftly over moss-covered rocks, was clear and sparkled in the sun. I knelt down and felt its mountain coldness.

From the bridge, the track climbed up again, into a copse of wild sumac. Jays hopped from branch to branch, their blue feathers brilliant against the dark foliage. At my approach, they began a disapproving chorus. I looked at them warily, because I have an unreasonable fear of birds, but kept going through the trees to a clearing.

The tall grass there had been bleached to a wheat color by the sun and was crushed and bent, as if a car had been driven in and parked there. To the right of the clearing was a tumbledown shed, its doors sagging on rusty hinges and most of its roof caved in.

Straight ahead, on still higher ground, stood what remained of Levin's cabin.

All that was standing was a cement-block foundation, a few charred beams, and a chimney of blackened stone. The lower branches of the redwood trees that shaded it had been burned, and their great trunks were badly scorched and splattered with a yellow substance that might have been a fire retardant. It was impossible to tell what the cabin had looked like, but from the foundation I could see that it had been little more than two rooms. I went up to it and stepped over the cement blocks to get a closer look.

The kitchen had been at the rear of the structure, as evidenced by a heat-blistered two-burner stove and refrigerator. A pair of galvanized pipes showed where the sink had stood. The basin itself lay on the ground, the cabinet that had held it having burned to ashes. Blackened porcelain fixtures indicated that the bathroom had been to the right of the kitchen. Near the stone fireplace lay the charred remains of springs and a mattress.

How had the fire started? I wondered. Faulty wiring? Sparks from the fireplace? Had Levin been smoking in bed? Or had he even been here at the time? I began walking around through the ashes and debris, looking for the blaze's origin.

I didn't know much about investigating the scenes of fires, but it seemed logical that the place of origin would be where the most damage was. The cabin, however, seemed uniformly burned. I assumed there was no fire department up here and that Levin had not been able to put the blaze out himself. Probably he had merely contained it and allowed it to burn itself out. That might account for the equal degree of destruction. Or maybe the fire had started in more than one place. I'd have to call a man I knew on the Arson Squad and ask him about that when I got back to the city.

I stepped up to the blackened foundation and surveyed my surroundings. To one side was a dense thicket where I could hear the creek splashing over the rocks. Behind the ruins was a dark ring of redwoods. The temperature under the trees was cool and the air was redolent with the scent of bay laurel. Under it, the smell of charred wood lurked like an unspoken warning.

I kicked at the foundation in frustration. There was nothing here that would tell me any more about Jerry Levin. Even if I got down and hand-sifted through these ashes, they would yield no information. But maybe someone in Boulder Creek had known the dead man; I'd go there after I explored the property a little more.

Stepping off the cement blocks, I went over to the redwood grove and started through it. On the other side was an open meadow, dotted with scrub oak. I crossed it and again found myself at the edge of a steep slope, looking down into a valley many hundreds of yards below.

There were buildings down there, a large stone one with a slate roof and several smaller ones. I could look down on top of them. A black van and a jeep stood in front of them, but there was no other sign of life.

What was it? I wondered. A ranch? I tried to orient myself. Possibly it was the winery that went with the vineyards I'd seen on the hill. Given its curves and switchbacks, the road could very well have brought me deceptively close to civilization. Perhaps if I found out how to get down to the buildings, the people to whom the van and jeep belonged would be able to tell me something about Levin and the fire.

Intending to go back to the MG, I turned again and headed across the meadow. I was only a few feet from the redwood grove when I heard a buzzing sound close by. I stopped—and then I heard the crack of the shot.

I froze, then dove for the cover of the trees. A second shot cracked, and then another.

I landed on my hands and knees just beyond the first line of trees. Quickly I crawled deeper into their shelter, trying to figure out from which direction the shots had come. It was completely quiet now; even the cries of the birds were stilled. I crouched there, shaken, clutching a tree trunk.

The silence went on for what seemed like forever. I strained my ears, but heard no one moving in the underbrush. The shots had come from close by; as near as I could tell, whoever had fired them was somewhere between me and the road where I'd left my car.

But who was it? Someone who now owned the land and didn't like trespassers? But the land wasn't posted or fully fenced. And didn't reasonable people warn you before shooting?

Of course, this didn't have to be a reasonable person.

I shivered, suddenly cold. The silence went on. I took the absence of bird calls to mean the sniper was still out there.

Was he waiting for me to make the next move? I could stay still, wait him out—but for how long? Until dark? That was hours away.

Slowly I began to move through the redwoods toward the ruins of the cabin. I stayed in a crouch, going from the trunk of one tree to another. When I got to the edge of the grove, I would have to run across open space to the ruins. It was only a short way, though, and once there I would have the foundation for protection. Then if I could get to the thicket by the creek—

Another shot rang out. I dropped to my stomach, cursing the pale pink blouse that made me easy to spot, even in the deep shade.

The shot, however, had helped me pinpoint its source: near the clearing on this side of the plank bridge. Possibly the sniper was using the tumbledown shed as cover.

After a few moments I began to move again, keeping as close to the ground as I could. If I could get to the thicket by the creek, I could wade across it and climb up the other bank to the road. The stand of sumac I'd come through earlier would screen my approach to the MG from anyone in the clearing by the shed. Providing the sniper hadn't found the car and disabled it—a frightening possibility—I would then get the hell out of here.

I was at the edge of the redwoods now. Several yards away stood the ruins of the cabin. If I could get across that seemingly immense space, the foundation and chimney would shield me.

I dashed out from the shelter of the trees, leaped over the foundation, and hurled myself behind the chimney just as a bullet smacked into the stone wall a mere three feet from me. The shot echoed and then died away.

Lying there on my stomach, my nose in the ashes, I felt pure rage rise up to supplant my terror. Dammit, no one had the right to play this deadly kind of game with another human being!

I began inching through the rubble, determined to get to that thicket. When I reached the other side of the foundation, I raised myself and peered over it, braced to duck a bullet. Everything remained silent. I supposed my black hair was not noticeable against the charred debris, but when I stood up and started running, I would make a clear target. Still, I had to get to the road. . . .

I leaped over the foundation and ran in a crouch for the protection of the thicket. Another shot sounded as I slid into the thicket on my knees. Stumbling to my feet, I fought through the underbrush, branches slapping my face and tearing at my clothes.

The creek was narrow at this point, and I waded into it, feeling the shock of the cold water through my tennis shoes. Then I was on the bank beyond, scaling the rocky slope that I hoped led to the road. I reached the top, gasping with relief when I saw the broken pavement.

Cautiously I stepped out a couple of inches and peered down the road. My car stood where I had left it. If the sniper had come across the countryside rather than along the road, there was a good chance he hadn't even seen it.

I began moving down the road in the shelter of the underbrush. Since the last shot, I had heard nothing. Pausing at the entrance to the rutted driveway, I listened. Silence. I sprinted across the entrance and kept going.

There was a crashing in the sumacs to my left. I stopped, half panicked, only a few feet from my car. A deer came leaping from the trees. It cleared the road in a single bound and disappeared.

Weak with relief, I closed my fingers around the car keys in my pocket. Then I ran for the MG and jumped in. I hunched low in the seat and jammed the keys into the ignition. The car started on the first try.

I let out the clutch and gunned the MG wildly down the road.

chapter twelve

Boulder Creek was a bigger town than I'd imagined. It was the gateway to Big Basin State Park, and its streets were crowded with vans and campers, even though it was only May. There were lines at the filling stations, and people with wilderness gear lugged boxes of supplies out of the grocery stores. Even the bars were jammed. I took one look at the confusion and decided to go back to San Francisco.

I probably should have reported the sniping incident to the local law, but I'd decided there was no point in it. The sniper would be long gone, and talking to the police and giving a statement would only cause me unnecessary delay. I headed toward the freeway and drove north, going over the incident in my mind, trying to make sense of it.

The person had definitely been shooting at me, but he hadn't been aiming to kill. None of the bullets had come very close to me; he'd have to have been an exceptionally poor shot to have missed me so many times. No, his intention had been merely to scare me. But why not shout a warning and save his ammunition? I still didn't understand.

Of course, the mountains down there had a reputation for harboring crazies. Bodies were frequently found in the wilderness and the nearby city of Santa Cruz had been dubbed, unofficially, the "murder capital of California," due to more than one series of mass murders. So maybe I'd just crossed paths with one of the resident lunatics.

The city, with fog boiling in over the hills, was a welcome sight. I exited the freeway at Army Street, remembered to keep going straight rather than turn toward my old apartment on Guerrero, and in minutes I was home. Don's gold Jaguar stood at the curb; I eased the MG in behind it.

He was in the living room, spackling the walls. When I came in he turned, wiping the putty knife on the tail of his old workshirt, a cheerful grin on his face. The grin faded when he saw me.

"What happened to you?"

I looked down at my jeans and pink blouse, which were grimy with soot.

Don waited.

"Somebody shot at me."

"What!"

"A sniper. I don't think he was trying to hit me, and I'm fine. Only a little dirty, that's all."

"Where did this happen?"

I told him, briefly, trying to minimize the seriousness of it. He listened, stroking his mustache. Finally he said, "You shouldn't have gone down there alone."

"I tried to call you, but you were out."

"You should have waited."

"Don, it's my job. I couldn't wait."

"Yeah. Your job." He turned away, set the putty knife down, and put the top back on the spackle.

I felt a sinking sense of *déjà vu*. This had happened before, with other men. "Don, please don't hate my job. It's the most important part of my life; I have to do it. If you hate it, you're also hating me."

"Oh, babe." He turned back, his face full of concern. "That's not it at all. I'm just worried because I love you."

Relief flooded through me. "I love you too."

That was the way it had been with us since the day we met: simple, easy. How could I have thought he'd be like the others? "How did your tour of the studios go?" I said. "Did they play your demo tape?"

"Yes, and liked it a lot, I think. The studios are terrific, too. I'd never realized what a small operation KPSM is. What I could do in those studios. . . ."

I felt a defensive tightening that was becoming all too familiar, followed by a flash of annoyance at myself. "Listen, Don," I said, "I want to take a bath. Then you can tell me all about it."

I spent close to an hour in the tub, periodically adding more hot water when the temperature cooled. I lay submerged, the ends of my hair trailing in the water, trying to make sense of this emotional rollercoaster ride. Finally, though, I had to get out and dry off. A bathtub is a good place to hide, but not indefinitely.

When I came into the kitchen Don was reading at the table. He shut the book immediately and poured us glasses of wine. Then he said, "Look, I think we should talk."

I pulled the belt of my robe tighter and sat down across from him. "About what?"

"About why you get so uptight every time I mention the job at KSUN. Is there some reason you don't want me to move to San Francisco?"

There. It was out in the open. "No. I'm happy for you. . . ."

"Is there somebody you're seeing here, and you feel my living in town would interfere with that?"

"Lord, no!"

"What is it then?"

I looked down into my wine. Don waited.

"I don't know."

"Maybe you should try to figure it out."

"Maybe." But I already had—the pictures that had drifted through my mind while I'd soaked in the tub had told me.

In the past two months, because they'd helped me move into this house, I'd helped two friends move out of theirs. Each had been breaking off with the man she'd lived with, and each moving day had been horrible. One man had pretended it didn't matter and had bustled around the house, rearranging what furniture was staying, talking about getting on with his life. The other had tried to help us, but had had to keep going off into another room to cry. I'd had plenty of time, while carting out boxes and taking pictures off the walls, to think about the death of relationships, the failure of love. To realize that hands that once touched you with tenderness could just as easily shove you away. To know that a voice once soft with passion could in time become edged with indifference or pain.

It seemed to me that relationships between men and women didn't last very long these days. And it also seemed that, the more you were together, the more you hastened that almost certain end.

What I had with Don was very precious and new. I didn't want to see it end—not ever. But what if being together more—as we would be if he lived here in town—caused it to turn into something less? What if . . .

"Don," I said, "I'm afraid—"

The phone rang. I gave it what must have been a murderous look. It rang again. Don squeezed my hand and said, "You better answer it."

Willie Whelan's voice came over the wire. "Sharon?"

"Yes, Willie." I glanced at Don. He was reaching for his book.

"I tried your office, but they said you'd been out all day. Where were you?"

"Getting shot at."

"What?"

I explained about my talk with David Halpert and Ben Cohen, and the resultant trip to the Santa Cruz Mountains.

"Jesus," he said. "You better be careful. No telling what kinds of lunatics are running around. But listen, the reason I called, I've got something for you."

"You found the Torahs?"

"No, but I know where they were."

"Where?"

"In with the rolls for the player piano."

Of course. To the untutored eye, they wouldn't look all that different. "How do you suppose they got there?"

"Somebody must have thought it was a good hiding place. And it sure fooled me. What I don't get, though, is who did it—or how he sneaked them in here."

"Does anyone have a key to your house?"

"No, ma'am. In my business you got to be real careful about things like that."

"I guess so. Wait a minute—you said they *were* in with the rolls. What happened to them?"

"It's like this: I came home and was going to hunt for them, like Zahn said you wanted me to. But first I fixed myself a sandwich and took it and a beer to the front room. I was just sitting down when I heard the door to the passageway open."

"The passageway?"

"You know that little door to the left of the garage door, as you're facing the house?"

I could picture it vaguely. "Yes."

"It opens into a passageway that leads to the backyard. There're gas and electric meters in there, and a second door that goes into the garage, back where my desk is."

"Okay. Go on."

"The door opened; it's never locked because the meter readers have to get in. I went to the window and looked down, but I didn't see anybody. So then I went to the garage, to make sure the other door was locked. And it wasn't."

"But no one was there?"

"Right. What I heard must have been somebody leaving. If he was standing right in the doorway when I looked out the front window, I couldn't have seen him."

"What did you do next?"

"Looked around the garage to see if anything was missing. It was real obvious someone had been in those player piano rolls because they were all over the floor. I picked one up and looked at it, and then I realized there had been a lot more in the box before. And *then* I realized some of the others had been longer than this one and had had those handles you described. I may be dumb, but not so dumb I couldn't put it together."

It was the perfect hiding place. Too bad neither of us had thought about it before someone had broken in and taken the Torahs. "Willie," I said, "I'm coming over there."

"Why? The Torahs are gone."

"Maybe he missed one. At any rate, I want to look over that passageway."

"Okay, I'm not doing anything but sitting around waiting for Alida to show up. She was supposed to be here a while ago, but for some reason she's late."

"See you in fifteen minutes." I replaced the receiver and started for the bedroom to change. Then I remembered Don. He hadn't looked up from his book.

I went over and put my hand on his shoulder. "I have to go out, but we'll talk more when I get back."

He covered my hand with his. "Don't worry, babe. It'll keep."

"But I think I can explain it now, and I want to—"

"We'll talk. Go do what you have to, and then we'll talk."

Again, it was so easy. Perhaps, when they were this simple and straightforward, some relationships could work. Perhaps.

It was fairly clear on my side of Twin Peaks, but when I reached the top of the Seventeenth Street hill, the fog rose up to meet me. It thickened as I descended into the area near the Medical Center. The streets were near-deserted and the little stores and cafés seemed like a backlit stage set, unreal and indistinct. I turned left on Carl Street and followed the red taillights of an N-Judah street-car along the tracks to where they turned at the top of Arguello.

Rounding the corner, I began looking for a parking space, then slowed almost to a stop. On the other side of the intersection red and blue lights flashed, their beams highlighting the walls of crumbling old Kezar Stadium. There were three patrol cars, an ambulance, and a crowd of onlookers. I took my foot off the brake and coasted down the hill, past Willie's house. The focus of the crowd's attention appeared to be under the cypress trees, close to the stadium.

I didn't like to rubberneck, so I found a parking space between a motorcycle and a fire hydrant. Then I got out of the car and stood on the sidewalk, debating about going down. I had just decided there was no sense in adding one more body to the confusion when a dark sedan pulled up and a familiar figure emerged—Leo McFate, adjusting the lapels of his three-piece suit.

McFate's presence meant a homicide—a second homicide in this vicinity in twenty-four hours. Coincidence? Maybe, but . . .

I started down the sidewalk, crossed the intersection, and stopped on the edge of the crowd, next to a tall black man in a ski parka. "What's happening?" I asked him.

"Looks like some woman got mugged."

A man in front of me turned and said, "It's a bad place to be walking at night. People do it anyway, though—cut across here toward the park. Although why any sensible woman would want to go into the park at this hour . . ."

I worked my way deeper into the crowd, toward the stadium. Normally it would have been pitch dark here under the thick cypress trees, but now floodlights illuminated the high walls of Kezar.

"God knows you won't catch me going out alone at night anymore," a woman beside me said to her male companion.

"What happened?" I asked again.

"I don't know if it was a rape or a mugging, but either way, she's dead."

I pushed forward. The crowd was a large one, probably nearby apartment dwellers and pedestrians who had been going to or from the Med Center. While the nighttime activity was focused at the top of Arguello, where the parking garages and streetcar stop were, the lights from the squad cars would have drawn people down here before the police had had a chance to cordon off the area. Now they were starting to move the people back.

I squeezed between two women and stepped into the front row of onlookers. The ambulance was pulled up near the ticket booth of the stadium and McFate stood next to it, talking to a patrolman. He held a fringed leather purse in his hand, and was taking a wallet from it.

A couple of white-coated medics knelt over a figure on the ground, near the trunk of one of the trees. She wore jeans, boots, and a tan corduroy jacket. I stepped forward and saw her long blond hair.

I started and put my hand to my mouth, then glanced back at McFate. He was reading the identification in the wallet. I took a couple more steps, close enough to see the woman's face, and felt my stomach tighten. The woman was Alida Edwards.

A patrolman blocked my way. "Stand back, ma'am. You can't go any closer."

I looked around him at Alida's body.

"Ma'am, please move."

I did as he told me.

Willie, I thought. I've got to tell Willie. He was up there at his house, waiting for both of us, and Alida was . . . I turned to go, but the people formed a solid mass behind me. A sudden motion in the crowd—some kind of scuffle—attracted my attention and I looked over to my right. As I did, my glance held on a face about twenty feet away.

Willie. Pale in the garish light, his expression bleak and hopeless.

I called his name. His head snapped around. Then his eyes narrowed and his jaw thrust out defiantly. He whirled and shouldered away through the crowd.

"Willie!"

I began pushing through the people behind me. They protested, some muttering obscenities, but I kept going. When I reached the intersection, Willie was halfway up the street, running toward his truck.

"Willie! Wait!"

He jumped in the truck without looking back. The engine roared, the headlights flashed, and he backed into the street. I ran uphill, still hoping to stop him. But it was too late. The tires squealed as he took off toward the Med Center and turned right on Irving.

chapter thirteen

I stood on the sidewalk, staring after Willie's truck. Why had he panicked and run off from me, of all people? Surely he hadn't killed Alida.

Or could he have? Just to pose an extremely hypothetical situation, what if Alida had gotten there right after he'd spoken with me? They might have quarreled, and he might have killed her . . . and then dragged her body down a well-traveled street, dumped it under the trees by Kezar, and stood around waiting for the police? Sure.

What had she been doing down there anyway? I wondered. It wasn't on the route she would have taken to Willie's house from her apartment. If she was driving, she would have come up Irving and probably parked in front of Willie's. If she was coming on the streetcar, she would have gotten off at the stop in front of the hospital parking garage. Even walking, she would not have approached his house from that direction.

Okay, she might have been coming from somewhere besides her apartment. But where? There was nothing down there except the park. Alida had impressed me as a streetwise lady—she wouldn't walk through Golden Gate Park alone at night.

But the important thing now was to find Willie. The police already knew Alida's identity; it would only be a matter of time before they connected the two of them. If Willie turned up missing when he was already out on bail for another murder charge, it would be rough for him.

Where had he gone? The only place I could think of was the Oasis Bar and Grill.

The Oasis was not nearly so crowded on this Monday night as it had been yesterday. I checked out the drinkers on the stools, then wandered toward the back. No Willie. The table where we'd sat beyond the potted palm was empty.

When I got to the pay phone I dug out a dime and called Hank at All Souls. There was a long silence after I told him what had happened.

Finally he said, "Damn him, anyway."

"Running like that *was* a pretty stupid move."

"Stupid? The man's gone insane. How am I supposed to defend him when he acts like that?"

"It won't be easy, unless I find him before the cops connect him with Alida. Do you think he'd go to a friend, maybe? Someone he could talk to?"

"Willie's basically a loner. He doesn't have many friends, except for Alida."

"You said the two of you were friends."

"That's different; it's based on something that happened long ago. But he'd never turn to me in a crisis—and even if he would, he's had plenty of time to show up here if he was going to."

"Well, what about his acquaintances from the flea markets? His runners? Would he go to them?"

"I don't know. I'm beginning to realize I don't know Willie anymore. You might as well try those people if you can find them."

"Okay, I'll check in later."

I hung up and took the phone book from the shelf. There were no listings for Roger Beck or Sam Thomas in San Francisco. Monty Adair, however, had an address in Pacific Heights. Mack Marchetti lived out in the Avenues, in the Sunset district. It wasn't much, but it was a place to start.

* * *

Monty Adair's building was a highrise on upper Broadway. It had an elegant marble facade to match the elegant neighborhood, and most of its windows would command a panoramic view of the Bay. I was surprised at first that a flea market vendor could afford such a place, but when I saw the number of mailboxes in the foyer, I realized the building was merely a rabbit warren of studio apartments, designed for people with not much money who wanted a good address. Each studio probably rented for as much as an entire house in my neighborhood, but there are any number of people who prefer putting on a front to living in comfort. I rang Adair's bell and he buzzed me in.

He was on the sixth floor, next to the elevator. When I stepped out of the car, the door to his apartment was already open. Adair stood in front of it, wearing jeans and a turtleneck, a thick book in his hand. A fleeting expression of surprise passed over his sharp features when he recognized me.

"Sharon, what can I do for you?" He made no move to invite me in.

"I was wondering if you'd heard from Willie in the past hour."

"Willie?" He rested the book on his hip. It looked like a college text, and on the far wall of the apartment, visible through the open door, were shelves that overflowed with similar volumes. "I thought Willie was in jail."

"He's out on bail." I debated telling him about Alida's murder, but decided it would take too much explaining and merely added, "I need to locate him, but he's not home. I thought he might be visiting you or one of his other friends."

"You'd never find him here."

"Oh?"

"Willie and I aren't friends. Business associates, yes. But not friends."

"I see. Do you know anyone he might visit?"

"Alida, of course. Maybe Sam."

"He's not with Alida. And I couldn't find an address for Sam. Do you know it?"

"No. He lives with a woman. Carolyn something. I can't recall her last name."

"Oh." I glanced down at the book he held, wondering if there was anything else I could ask him that might help me. The book was a history of World War II, and must have run at least eight hundred pages. "Heavy reading," I said. "Are you a student?"

"Not in the literal sense. I don't go to school. But I read a lot of history and political science."

"That looks like more than I'd tackle for an evening's entertainment."

"I guess most people would feel that way. But I look at it like this, Sharon: In order to get ahead in this world, you have to understand why it is the way it is. The best method of doing that is to understand the past."

"That's very interesting."

"Yes. Perhaps it's one reason Willie and I aren't friends. He doesn't attempt to understand or control things. He's not going anywhere. All he does is exist from day to day."

"And you are going somewhere?"

"Very definitely."

"Well, in the meantime, if you hear from Willie, would you tell him to call me?"

Adair nodded, his white scalp showing through his clipped hair. "I'll tell him."

"Thanks."

Adair's door was closed before I could ring for the elevator. I paused, realizing I should have asked him where I could reach Roger Beck. The hell with it, I decided; I'd ask Mack Marchetti and, if the flea market vendor didn't know, I'd call Adair later.

Unlike Adair, Marchetti clearly did not believe in putting on a front. The yard of his small stucco house on Twenty-seventh Avenue was weed-choked and sun-browned, and the house itself was badly in need of repair. Although a faint light shone behind the shade on the front room window, it was at least three minutes before Marchetti responded to my knock. When he did he just stood there, staring at me. He wore a plaid bathrobe and his iron-gray crewcut was wet and slicked down, as if he had just gotten out of the shower.

"I'm Sharon McCone, Mr. Marchetti. One of Willie Whelan's runners."

"Oh, yes. I saw you with him on Sunday. Somebody—Selena Gonzalez, I think—told me he had hired another person."

"I wonder if I could talk with you for a few minutes."

"What about?"

"Willie."

He glanced down at his robe. "Will it take long?"

"As I said, just a few minutes."

"All right. Let me change first, though." He opened the door wider and I followed him into a living room that was furnished with a cheap suite you might have found at one of the discount outlets on Mission Street. Its plaid upholstery clashed violently with Marchetti's robe.

"Make yourself at home; I'll be right back." He went off down the hallway.

I stood looking around. The couch, two chairs, and coffee table were arranged formally in front of a small fireplace. The lamps on the end tables were green ceramic and reminded me of the kind you always see in motels. I have a theory about these motel lamps: They are made as ugly as possible to discourage people from stealing them. The only attractive lamp I've ever seen in a motel room was bolted down.

The surfaces of the tables were empty except for a layer of dust. There were no magazines, pictures, books, or knick-knacks. The only personal object in the room, in fact, was not exactly a homey touch; it was a glass-fronted cabinet full of hunting rifles and shotguns. I went over to take a closer look. There was a lone handgun in the case, probably a .45 caliber military-type pistol, but there was something odd about it. I was still trying to figure it out when Marchetti came back, fully dressed.

"You like my collection?"

I turned. "It's impressive, if you're into hunting. I was wondering, what's this one here, the handgun?"

"Nel-Spot 007. You know what it's for?"

"No, what?"

"They use it on ranches for marking stock. The Forestry Service also uses it. It's carbon-dioxide powered, shoots pellets loaded with paint. You hit your target, the pellet breaks, and you've got your marking."

"Interesting. Have you worked on ranches?"

"As a matter of fact—"

The phone rang. "Excuse me a minute." Marchetti picked up the receiver and said, "Yeah?"

I sat down on one of the plaid chairs. Marchetti listened intently for a moment. "I see. That's bad news, terrible. . . . No, I haven't . . . I didn't . . . Sure, certainly . . . Okay, thanks." He replaced the receiver and turned to me, his face solemn. "That was Selena Gonzalez. Alida Edwards was murdered tonight."

"Good Lord," I said, feigning surprise.

He sat down on the couch, shaking his head. "A shame. A god-damned shame. She was a lovely girl."

"How did Selena hear about it?"

"On the radio."

I looked at my watch. It was ten-fifteen; the story would have just made the ten o'clock news broadcast. "How did Alida die?"

"She was stabbed in the neck."

I shuddered. "How's Selena taking it? Is she very upset?"

"Hard to say. She gets pretty dramatic. You never know what's real and what's for show. She says they've got an APB out on Willie."

It didn't surprise me; McFate had his faults but he worked quickly and efficiently. "I'm trying to find Willie myself."

"Why?"

"Personal reasons."

"Well, I don't know where he is. Do you think he killed Alida?"

"No."

"I don't believe he did either. He was crazy about the woman." He paused. "For an employee, you're mighty sure of your boss's innocence, though."

"I'm also Willie's friend. And I care what happens to him." As I said it, I realized it was true. In spite of my disapproval of his occupation, I genuinely liked the fence. Probably the feeling had started when I watched him convince Sam Thomas to see a doctor and have the bill sent to him. Certainly it had grown when I saw him take McFate down a peg. Whatever the reason, right now I might be the best friend Willie had.

"Why did you think Willie might be here?" Marchetti asked.

"I'm just checking all his friends and acquaintances—anyone I can think of."

He nodded.

"Can I check back with you later, in case he shows up?"

"You can, but I doubt it will do any good. Willie won't come here—especially with the police looking for him."

"Why not?"

"Let's just say he and I don't see eye-to-eye."

"About what?"

"Everything. Never have."

"Can you give me an example?"

"It's between Willie and me."

Strange that both Adair and Marchetti didn't get along with Willie; the fence was such an amiable man that I found it hard to understand. "Mr. Marchetti, can you at least give me addresses and phone numbers for Willie's other two runners? I've already talked to Monty Adair, but I don't know how to reach Roger Beck or Sam Thomas."

He went to the table where the phone was and took out an address book. "I happen to have them, since the runners sometimes spell Willie at the Saltflats. I like to be able to reach all the people who sell regularly at my market." Paging through the book, he read off an address in Oakland for Beck, and one here in the city, on Forty-ninth Avenue, for Thomas.

I copied them down, thanked him, and left. The address for Sam Thomas was not far away, near the Great Highway and the beach. From what I'd seen, Willie was friendlier with Thomas than with Beck. I decided to stop at Sam's first.

chapter fourteen

The fog was blowing in off the ocean when I arrived at Forty-ninth Avenue; it poured over the tops of the sand dunes and rushed across the Great Highway. There was a construction area across the street from Sam Thomas's house—part of a big sewer project that had been underway for several years—and the heavy equipment and piles of pipe loomed dark in the swirling mist.

When I got out of my car, gritty particles of sand stung my face. Narrowing my eyes against it, I looked up and down the street for Willie's truck. It wasn't there, but if he was at Sam's he wouldn't park close by; after all, he must know the police were looking for him. I locked the car and went up to the address Marchetti had given me. It was a shabby frame bungalow, its white paint pitted by sand.

The front of the house was dark, but light streamed out from a side window. I knocked and waited, hearing nothing but the roar of the surf and the howl of the wind. Then there were footsteps, the door opened, and Sam Thomas stood silhouetted in the doorway. He was dressed as he had been at the flea market, in jeans and a T-shirt, and he reeked of beer.

"Sharon. What are you doing here?" He spoke slowly, giving precise pronunciation to each word.

"I'm looking for Willie."

"He's gone."

"Then he *was* here?"

"Until about half an hour ago."

"Damn!"

A voice spoke behind Sam. "Who is it, honey?" Then a face appeared to his right: a lovely oval framed by straight black hair.

"It's Sharon McCone, the detective," Sam said to her. "Sharon, this is my lady, Carolyn Bui."

She stepped forward and looked me over, then extended her hand. "Come in, please. It's cold with the door open."

We went through a darkened living room to a yellow kitchen that was carpeted in a hypnotic black-and-white pattern. A table extended from one wall and around it were three director's chairs. I could tell where Sam had been sitting by the open can of beer. Opposite it was a mug of coffee.

Carolyn motioned for me to take the third chair. In this light I could appreciate her diminutive features and delicately up-tipped eyes. Not Chinese, I decided; more likely Southeast Asian or perhaps Eurasian.

"Willie told you I was a detective?" I asked.

Sam sat down and picked up his beer. "He said there wasn't much point in hiding it anymore."

"No. It wasn't a very good idea to begin with."

Carolyn took her mug to the stove. "Coffee?" she asked.

"Please." I could use some; it looked like it would be a long night.

Sam crumpled his beer can and tossed it into a plastic trash basket, where it joined dozens of others. Reaching behind him, he opened the refrigerator and took out another. He seemed high, but not drunk; probably he was one of those people who—when they want to—can maintain a certain level of mild intoxication throughout the day.

Carolyn set the coffee in front of me and joined us. "You're looking for Willie?"

"Yes. When did he get here?"

Sam looked at a big clock on the wall over the table. "Around nine, maybe. He was in bad shape, man. I gave him a few beers. Carolyn tried to make him eat, but he wouldn't."

"And then?"

"We sat around and talked, mostly about Alida. About the guy who got shot in his garage. And then, all of a sudden, he decided to split."

"Why?"

"Don't know."

Carolyn said, "I think he didn't want to get us in trouble by staying here. Willie's a very thoughtful man."

Sam glanced at her and then looked away. "I doubt it even crossed his mind, at a time like that."

"He left out of consideration for us."

"Look, I know Willie better than you do—"

"Sam."

He shrugged and drank some beer.

"Did he say where he planned to go?" I asked.

"No," Carolyn said.

"Do you have any guesses where he might be?"

"A motel, maybe. He took Sam's van and left his truck hidden in our garage."

"Oh, come on, honey," Sam said. "The man's wanted by the police. He's not just going to walk into some motel."

"He might."

Again Sam fell silent.

"What about other people he might have gone to?" I said. "I've already talked to Monty Adair and Mack Marchetti. Neither of them felt he would seek them out, but surely there must be someone—"

Sam laughed shortly. "You can bet he wouldn't go near either of them. Willie hates Marchetti, thinks he's a fascist. Adair—well, he doesn't trust him."

Personally, I didn't trust the cold-eyed vendor either, but I asked, "Why?"

"Monty's real anxious to get ahead. And he's smart. Willie respects him for his mind, but he's not too sure Monty wouldn't use his brains to screw him if he could. So he watches him real careful."

"Monty's too smart to try to cheat Willie," Carolyn said.

"You never know."

"He would never risk it."

Sam reached for another beer. I was beginning to get an idea of how this household operated, and I was also liking Carolyn a whole lot less. Her constant overruling of Sam's opinions couldn't be very good for someone whose self-esteem was already low.

"What about Roger Beck?" I asked. "Would Willie go to him?"

Sam smiled slyly. "Not hardly."

"I sensed they weren't friends when I went down to the San Jose market with Willie."

"You got it. There's woman trouble there, bad woman trouble."

"You mean, Willie took somebody away from Roger?"

"The opposite."

"What? I can't believe that."

"It's true. Willie's ex-wife divorced him so she could marry Rog. She hated Willie's business, said he ignored her and spent all his time in the garage or down at the Oasis with a bunch of thieves. She told Willie that Rog was sensitive and understood her needs. *I* think Rog was available and a good way to hurt Willie. Anyway, it didn't last long; within a year she ran off with some salesman. I tell you, when Willie heard about that, it made his whole year."

I remembered the way the fence had needled Beck about his wife leaving him—and how Beck had just stood there and taken it.

"Willie's business has caused him plenty of woman trouble," Sam went on. "Take Alida—she could never face up to the fact he was a fence. She'd say, 'Willie's a perfectly legitimate businessman,' and then she'd give you that prissy look of hers that would dare you to say otherwise."

"You shouldn't talk about her that way now," Carolyn said.

"Well, she *was* prissy. Her being dead doesn't change that."

"Still, it isn't nice."

"*Alida* wasn't nice, sometimes."

"Sam!"

He lapsed into silence, staring moodily at the top of his beer can.

I looked at the big clock. It was close to eleven-thirty. "So Willie came here around nine and stayed until roughly ten-thirty?"

"Yes." Carolyn got the coffee pot and refilled our cups.

"And you talked mainly about Alida."

"He kept telling us how he was standing in his front window, wondering why she was late," she said. "He saw the lights from the police cars at the corner and people going down there. So he decided to find out what had happened. You can imagine how he felt when he saw her lying there."

"Did he have any idea who might have killed her?"

"He said there had been a prowler in his house, someone who took those Torahs the man who got shot was looking for. He figured Alida came along, saw the guy leaving, and followed him."

It was a possibility. "But why would she follow him alone, rather than get Willie to go with her?"

"That was Alida's way of doing things. She was very independent."

"Stubborn," Sam said.

Carolyn glared at him.

"Willie has this idea that the same person who shot the guy in his garage killed Alida," Sam said. After a pause, he added, "For such a little wimp, that guy caused a lot of trouble."

Carolyn looked sharply at him. "I think 'trouble' is too mild a word for it."

He shrugged. "Think of him, though: scrawny, half bald, couldn't have weighed over a hundred pounds wet, running around decked out like he was on his way to a funeral—"

"Sam," I said, "when did you see Levin?"

"Oh, I guess it was about a week ago."

"Did he come to the Alameda market?"

"No. It was in David's Deli, downtown in the theater district. I was walking by and he and Selena Gonzalez were at a table in the front window. Heads together over their sandwiches, real cozy. I thought it was funny—Selena thinks she's quite a woman, and there she was with this wimp in a skullcap. So I stopped and tapped on the glass. Gave her a scare. But then she got mad and made motions for me to scram. I went—I don't like to mess too much with a crazy broad like Selena. You never know what she'll do."

No, I thought, you certainly don't. "Sam, did you tell Willie about this?"

"Not until tonight. I'd forgotten about it until he started talking about this Levin. You know, maybe that was what made him take off; he asked a whole lot of questions and then he left."

I stood up, nearly knocking my coffee over.

Both Sam and Carolyn looked surprised. "You taking off too?" he asked.

"Yes. Thanks for the coffee. I'll be in touch."

Now that I'd heard Sam's story about Levin and Selena, I thought I knew where Willie had gone. And I wanted to catch up with him in a hurry. Willie might be smart, and he might be tough, but he was an amateur at the business of detection.

chapter fifteen

When I'd been at Alida's the previous night, Selena had said she lived next door on the ground floor and had motioned at the north wall of the apartment. That meant her building was the Spanish-style stucco two doors from the corner. It was a house, but there was a small entry to one side of the garage, and Selena's name was on a mailbox next to it. Probably what she had was an in-law apartment.

There was no knocker or buzzer, so I tried the knob. The door swung open into a narrow passageway similar to the one Willie had described at his house. It was dark in there, and the damp air smelled of cats, but at the far end I could hear rock music and see a shaft of light spilling from under another door. I felt my way back there and knocked hard, hoping to be heard above the music.

In a few seconds the volume decreased and Selena's voice said, "Who is it?"

"Sharon McCone. I need to talk to you."

"Go away. It's late."

"I have to talk now. It's important."

"I was asleep. Come back tomorrow."

How could she sleep with that music playing? "Please; it can't wait."

There was a pause and then I heard a deadbolt turn. Selena's face peered over a security chain. Her thick hair tumbled down around her shoulders, and her face was pale, her eyes red. She stared at me for a moment, then unhooked the chain and let me in.

The apartment was only one room, the small kitchen separated from the rest of it by a formica counter. A couple of rickety-looking stools stood in front of it and there was a mattress on the floor in one corner, but otherwise the place was devoid of furnishings. Selena, who was wrapped in a multicolored afghan, regarded me for an instant and then went to the counter and turned the radio up again. A raucous jingle announced that KSUN was "the light of the Bay," and then the disc jockey began babbling about a sixties nostalgia party.

I resented the notion of the sixties as nostalgia. After all, I could *remember* the sixties; I had been almost an adult then. And the station sounded even more frantic than KPSM, where Don worked in Port San Marco. Why couldn't he be offered a job at a decent station, for Lord's sake?

Selena sat down on the mattress, pulling the afghan closer around her. In spite of its protection, she shivered. I took a good look at her and realized she was not only upset, but scared. Perching on one of the rickety stools, I said, "Are you okay?"

She shrugged.

"I know it must have been an awful shock about Alida."

She started to speak, but it came out a croak, and she cleared her throat. "It was horrible. To hear it that way, on the radio. She was so young and alive, and now this. It makes me wonder when they will come for me."

"They?"

"Death's messengers."

Marchetti had said she was dramatic, and he'd been right. "I wouldn't worry, Selena. You're safe here."

"There is no safety anywhere in this world."

I didn't want to argue with her; she was probably right. "Did Willie come here tonight?"

The shift in subject startled her. "How did you know? He was like a madman. Grief . . ."

"Grief and suspicion. Sam Thomas told him about seeing you with Jerry Levin."

"I know." She shivered again and pulled the afghan tighter.

The loud music was beginning to set me on edge. "Selena, can I turn this radio down?"

"No, leave it. It keeps the demons away."

Demons, madmen, death's messengers—what next? I raised my voice and began to talk over the sound. "Why did you meet with Jerry Levin that day, Selena?"

"I knew him a little bit."

"But you pretended you didn't."

She looked down at the granny squares that covered her lap.

"What were you and Levin talking about that day, when Sam saw you at David's Delicatessen?"

"We . . . I was trying to help him."

"Help him how?"

She was silent.

"How?"

She looked up, tears in her eyes, then covered her face with her hands. I suspected it was merely more dramatics, so I got down off the stool, snapped the radio off, and went to stand over her.

"All right, Selena. You can tell me about it now, or you can get dressed and come to the Hall of Justice with me and talk to a Homicide inspector I know. He's not a very nice man, and he's likely to be a lot rougher on you than I am. He might even start asking questions about your status with Immigration."

She took her hands away from her face. The tears were gone, and her eyes flashed with fury. "You and everyone else! Always threatening me with the Immigration. People are always forcing me to do things I don't want to—"

"Selena, what did you and Levin talk about?"

She jumped up, stalked to the counter, and turned the radio back on. Then she stood against the ledge, afghan gathered defiantly around her.

"All right! I will tell you, but only to keep out of trouble with the Immigration. Willie had something belonging to Jerry Levin. And Jerry Levin wanted it back. That is all."

"Do you mean the Torahs?"

"Yes."

"And you were going to help Levin get them back?"

"I did not say yes or no. He wanted me to get him the keys to Willie's house. I said I would think about it."

"And did you get them?"

"No."

"Are you sure?"

"Yes, I am sure!"

"Did Levin say how the Torahs had gotten into Willie's hands?"

"No. He said Willie had them. He wanted them back so he could return them to their rightful owners."

"Did he tell you he was from something called the Torah Recovery Committee?"

"The what? I have never heard of such a thing."

"He didn't mention it?"

"No. All he said was that he had to right a wrong."

I sat down on the edge of the mattress. "What kind of wrong?"

"He had committed a crime against his people. Many crimes. I think he meant he had stolen those Torahs. And he had used the fruits of his misdeeds to further a false cause. Then, later on, he rediscovered his faith, and he knew he must set the thing right."

"By giving back the Torahs?"

"Yes. He had rediscovered his faith while he was alone in the wilderness. He used those exact words—'alone in the wilderness.' And when his enemies tired to destroy him, he knew he must atone for what he had done."

Levin's story was as melodramatic as Selena herself. I wondered if he had been putting on an act for her benefit. The man seemed to have been able to adapt his poses to the people he was dealing with. If he'd sensed that Selena was a superstitious Old World Catholic, he might have used the ploy of repentance in order to enlist her sympathies. Or, oddly enough, he might have been telling the truth.

"So he asked you to steal Willie's keys for him," I said.

"Yes. I said I would think about it, but I had no intention of doing so."

"Did he ask you to do anything else for him?"

"No. He merely talked of his religion and how he had rediscovered his faith. It was very interesting to me."

"I'm sure it was. How did you and Levin get together in the first place?"

She looked away from me. "What do you mean?"

"How did he approach you? How did you meet?"

"Oh, he bought some dried apricots from me and then began talking."

But from the look on her face, I knew she was lying. "About what? His religion?"

"No. About . . . about the fruit."

"What about it?"

"It . . . it was particularly good. The fruit, you know, must be dried under certain conditions—"

"I am going to ask you again: How did you meet Levin?"

"I told you!"

"Are you sure you told the truth?"

"Yes!" She stamped her foot. "Why do you doubt me? Why does everyone doubt me?"

"There's probably a good reason for that."

She looked at me, her lower lip trembling. When confronted, cry.

In a moment I said, "Did you tell Willie all this when he came here tonight?"

"Yes. He was like a madman, yelling at me and shaking me. You would think *I* had killed Alida."

"Did you?"

Instead of the rage I expected, her face twitched with sadness. One hand moved involuntarily in the sign of the cross. "I loved Alida. She was the only person here who was really nice to me. I would never have done anything to hurt her."

"Someone did, though."

"Yes. I am afraid. . . ."

"Of what?"

"Of death. It has touched me. And I feel guilt."

"Why?"

"I . . . I should have been a better friend."

"That wouldn't have helped her."

"No, but it would have helped me."

I couldn't think of an answer.

"Are you through with your questions now?" she asked.

"Almost. Do you know where Willie was going when he left here?"

"No. He was calmer, and he looked very tired. Possibly he was going home to sleep."

But he wouldn't have, because he would know the police would be watching his house. "And he said nothing about his plans?"

"No." Selena went to the door and unhooked the chain, then unlocked the deadbolt. It was a strong one, and there was another below the doorknob. I remembered how she'd said she was afraid of living alone in a ground-floor apartment. She'd bought a gun from Fat Herman for protection. . . .

"Selena," I said, "why didn't you have your gun handy when you answered my knock? You said last night that you'd bought one for protection."

Her face paled. "I did. I had a gun—until tonight."

"What happened to it?"

"Do you remember what Alida said—that the gun could be taken away from me?"

"Yes."

"She was right. It was taken. By Willie."

chapter sixteen

I liked the idea of Willie running around with Selena's gun even less than I liked the idea of him playing amateur detective. Although the .22 was what Fat Herman referred to as "a plinker," it was just as lethal as my own .38. And while Willie had undoubtedly handled weapons in Vietnam, armed combat in a war zone was very different from a personal vendetta here in the streets of San Francisco.

I left Selena's apartment and drove the few blocks to Willie's house. While logic dictated that he wouldn't have returned there after hearing about the APB, I told myself that his actions up to this point hadn't been exactly rational. The old van that I remembered Sam having at the flea market was nowhere in sight, however. There was a vehicle that looked like an unmarked police car parked at the corner.

Where now? I wondered. Roger Beck was the last of Willie's acquaintances I knew, and, as Sam had said, it was unlikely the fence would show up on Beck's doorstep. Perhaps Selena was right; Willie had been tired and had gone some place to sleep. He could have parked the van in any number of spots throughout the city and climbed into the back to rest. At any rate, it wouldn't do me any good to continue driving around looking for him.

I headed home to Church Street.

There were lights on in my living room, but the house was quiet except for a crackling sound that I identified as coming from my stereo speakers. I went in there and turned the set off, then noticed Don asleep on the couch. His knees were drawn up like a child's and there was a hole in one of his socks. I felt a wave of tenderness and stood watching him for a moment before I touched his shoulder. He jerked and looked at me, hazel eyes unfocused.

"Were you waiting up for me?" I said.

"I was, but obviously I didn't succeed." He struggled to a sitting position and looked at his watch. "Jesus, it's almost one o'clock. The last I remember it was nine-thirty."

"What'd you do—fall asleep listening to music?"

"If you can call it that. I was taping the evening show on KSUN, so I could study their format." He glanced at the stereo. "The tape's run out."

"Why were you doing that?"

"To get a feel for how they handle their programs."

"You *want* a show of yours to sound like that?"

"Not exactly." He yawned. "I'm hoping there's something new or different that I could do, within the established format."

"Anything would help. From what I've heard, that station is loud and obnoxious and caters to people with the mentality of a twelve year old." Even to myself, I sounded prickly and out of sorts.

Don stood up, frowning. "Have you had a bad night?"

"Yes."

"Do you want to talk about it?"

"No."

"Do you want to talk about us?"

"Not now."

"Then I'm going to bed." He started across the room, but paused in the doorway. "But babe, we've got to talk soon."

I was silent.

"This job possibility means a lot to me," he added. "I'm happy about it, and I hoped you would be, too. Let's not spoil it for both of us."

He went into the bedroom and I sat down on the couch. Didn't he understand how rough my night had been? Didn't he know how difficult it was dealing with yet another murder?

Of course he didn't. I hadn't even told him about Alida.

Wearily I reached for the phone and called my answering service; I'd switched over to it when I'd left for Willie's, since Don had said he wasn't expecting any calls and I didn't want him to have to bother with taking my messages. Hank had called twice. While 1:00 A.M. wasn't too late to get back to him—my boss existed on a minimal amount of sleep and was sure to be up and about—I decided it could wait until morning.

As I was about to hang up, the operator said, "Wait, I've got something else for you."

I could hear pieces of paper shuffling. In the last couple of months there had been a big personnel turnover at the service. Add that to the fact that the owner, Claudia James, who usually took the late-night shift, was on vacation, and you had pure chaos. I was amazed I'd gotten any messages at all.

"Here it is. Willie called."

I sat up straighter. "When?"

"Right at midnight. He said he didn't do it, but he's going to find out who did."

"Terrific."

"Does that make sense?"

"Yes and no." The message did, the course of action didn't.

"Did he say anything else?"

"That's it."

"Thanks." I hung up, then dialed the Oasis Bar and Grill. When a male voice answered, I said, "I want to leave a message for Willie."

"For . . . hold on." There were noises as if he was moving the phone to a more private place. "Okay, but I can't guarantee he'll get it."

"I know. If he comes in or calls, tell him Sharon got his message. I want him to get in touch with me right away. He's to do nothing until he talks to me."

There was a pause, and then the man read the message back to me. I thanked him and hung up.

I reached for the lamp on the end table and turned it out, then propped my feet on a hassock and sat there in the dark, my thoughts moving from Willie to Don, and back and forth again. Willie—there was nothing I could do about him. He would either call or not. Don, however . . .

I was treating Don badly, that I knew. And I was trying to use my job as an excuse for it. Now I knew why I was doing it, but I still couldn't stop myself.

The trouble was, I was afraid.

I'd been afraid many times before. This afternoon when I'd been shot at; once when I'd almost been stabbed to death; the time I'd had to kill a man because a friend's life depended on it. But that was gut-level physical fear; in response to it you took immediate action. I'd never been afraid on an emotional level, where feelings that I hardly understood made me incapable of action.

I told myself I had to get this fear under control. I'd better talk it out with Don before it fed on itself and destroyed everything the two of us had. Because it could very well do that—and losing him was one thing I didn't think I could face.

He'd been asleep when I crawled into bed long after three in the morning, and was already up when I woke at nine. I lay contemplating the cracks in the ceiling and thinking about guns—specifically Selena's.

The Mexican woman had lied to me about how she became acquainted with Levin, of that I was certain. Why wouldn't she also have lied about Willie taking her gun? Hank had told me Willie seemed to recognize the .22 with the chip out of its grip that had been used to shoot Levin. What if he'd known it was Selena's? What if the reason she didn't have it anymore was because she— or someone close to her—had left it in the garage after the killing?

Don appeared in the bedroom door, dressed in a sports coat, unlikely attire for his casual taste. "I'm going downtown to meet some of the people at KSUN," he said. "And then I'm having lunch with my friend Tony. I'll be back by mid-afternoon."

"I'll probably be home for dinner. If not I'll call you."

"Maybe we'll go out."

"Okay."

He turned and left abruptly, without giving me his usual good-bye kiss. While his words had been cordial, his face had looked a little pinched, as it did on the infrequent occasions when he was depressed. Dammit, why was I spoiling everything!

I got up, pulled my robe on, and called Hank. He sounded worried and irritated. "Where the hell have you been? I left three messages with your service last night."

"I only got two of them. And I got home very late."

"You should have called anyway. I swear—living with that guy is making you act like you have three brain cells."

"I'm not living with him. He's a guest."

"We'll see."

"What does that mean?"

"Nothing. You find out anything about Willie?"

I told him about Willie's message and what little else I knew. "I take it he hasn't given you a call?"

"Not a word."

"Hank, do you think you could find out some things about Levin's murder from McFate?"

"I'll try. What do you need?"

"I'm interested in the murder weapon, the twenty-two you thought Willie might have recognized. Find out the manufacturer and the type. If it was a High Standard Sentinel Deluxe, we might have a lead."

"Okay. Anything else?"

"Get all the details you can, both on Levin's murder and Alida's. If McFate won't talk to you, try someone else on Homicide."

"You mean like Greg?" There was a teasing note in Hank's voice.

I glared at the receiver, wishing he could see my displeasure. "Yes, like Greg." Why did Hank have to needle me about my boyfriends—both past and present?

I hung up the phone and went to the kitchen for a cup of coffee. The day was sunny and warm, so I took my mug to the back porch and sat on the steps. Watney leaped out from the tangle of an old, overgrown rose bush to the right of the little cement pathway and twittered at me, then leapt out of sight again. I stared at the hole into which he had disappeared. Watney was unusually vocal, but he had never been much of a twitterer. A yowler, but never a twitterer. Maybe having a backyard to stalk through would improve his rather vitriolic nature. After all, it must look like an absolute wilderness to him. . . .

Wilderness. I thought of Jerry Levin's remarks to Selena, about having rediscovered his faith in the wilderness and deciding to right the wrong he had done after his enemies tried to destroy him. Melodrama, for sure, but it might be based on reality. I went back inside, got my address book, and called Jack Foxx, a man I knew on the Arson Squad. Jack listened to my description of the destruction at Levin's cabin site and then said, "The fire could very well have been set. With most fires—whether they're accidental or arson—you can pinpoint a source. What you describe sounds like someone could have poured a flammable liquid throughout the structure and then ignited it. There's no way to tell, of course, without going over the scene."

I thanked Jack, promised to buy him a drink soon, and hurried to take my shower and dress. While I stood under the rushing water, I thought of Jerry Levin and his supposed enemies. If someone had really tried to burn his cabin, had that person—or persons—been trying to kill him? Not likely; if they'd spread gasoline around inside, they would have known he wasn't there. Scare him, then? Probably, but why? To make him stop searching for the seven missing Torahs? That didn't seem likely either. From what Ben Cohen had told me of the findings of the committee's investigators, Levin hadn't been looking for the Torahs at the time his cabin burned. It was only after he moved to the hotel in San Francisco's Tenderloin that he began haunting the flea market.

I decided to drop the knotty matter of Levin's motivations for a while and concentrate on the murder weapon. Hank might be a long time in getting the information I'd requested from the police. In the meantime, I could talk to Fat Herman.

*   *   *

The little shop on Mission Street was empty this morning, except for the genial fat man, who sat in the same place he'd occupied yesterday. He smiled when he saw me and stood up. "You decided to take that gun?"

"No."

"Why not? It's a good deal."

"I'm sure it is, but I already have one of my own. And I'm afraid I haven't been completely honest with you." I took my wallet out and showed him the photostat of my license.

Herman's smile faded. "Private cop, huh? Who are you working for?"

"Willie."

"Doing what?"

"Originally I was to find out why the man who was shot in his garage was following him. Now I'm trying to prove Willie didn't kill either Jerry Levin or Alida Edwards."

"Alida." Herman sat down again. "That was one hell of a thing."

"Are you willing to help me—and help Willie?"

He paused. "I'll do what I can. No guarantees, though. I got a business to protect."

"I understand. You told me yesterday that you sold a gun to Selena Gonzalez. Can you describe it, in detail?"

A strange look passed over his fleshy face. "I already did. High Standard Sentinel Deluxe. Nine-shot."

"I'm interested in anything peculiar about it."

"Like what?"

But I wanted him to remember whether there was a chip out of the grip by himself. "Anything that would distinguish it from another gun of the same type."

"You mean, was the grip chipped."

"Yes," I said, surprised.

"No."

"Then why did you mention it?"

Herman's face returned to its usual jovial set. "Because it looks like Willie's doing your job for you, little girl."

"What does that mean?"

"He was in here not an hour ago. You should see him—somewhere he's gotten hold of a beat-up raincoat and a ratty felt hat and some of the most holey shoes you'd ever hope to see. No one would recognize him as the king of the flea market. Fits right in with the rest of the derelicts around here."

Dammit, Willie was carrying this detective business too far! "Did he ask you about the gun with the chipped grip?"

"Yeah, but he didn't ask if it was Selena's. Wanted to know if I'd ever sold one like that to anyone he knew, though. And it wasn't a High Standard; it was an RG-14, your Saturday Night Special. Willie's ahead of you, girl. He knew its make."

I ignored the dig and said, "*Had* you sold it to anyone he knew?"

"Yes."

"Who?"

"That little runner of his, Monty Adair."

Monty. He wanted to get ahead in the world. Obviously he felt it required the help of a gun.

"Why did he buy it, did he say?"

"No."

"When was this?"

"About a year ago."

"Do you remember every gun you sell for that long?"

"Naw, but this one I do because I've seen a lot of Monty lately."

"At the flea market, or here in your store?"

"Both. That lad is real interested in guns."

"What's he bought from you?"

"Nothing. I didn't have what he was looking for. I'm not a member of the Krupp family." He chuckled. "And I didn't send him to the competition; I figured he's a smart kid, he can make his own way in the world."

I was certain of that. "Did you tell Willie all this?"

"Oh, yes. He was most interested."

"How did he react—angry, upset, what?"

Herman's smile grew wider, his eyes almost disappearing into the surrounding fleshy pouches. "Cold, little girl. Cold and furious."

chapter seventeen

In the morning light, Monty Adair's Pacific Heights highrise looked even less elegant; the marble facade was grimy and advertising circulars littered the floor of the foyer. I rang Adair's apartment, and when I didn't receive an answer, pressed another buzzer at random. After two more tries, the door lock was tripped and I went inside and took the elevator to the sixth floor.

The hallway was empty. I went up to Adair's door and knocked. There was no sound within. I knocked again, harder, and as I waited I glanced down. There were fresh gouges in the wood of both the door and frame that looked as if someone had been kicking them. I didn't remember seeing them last night.

Behind me I heard another door open, and a woman's strident voice said, "I told you to go away. If you don't, I'm calling the cops."

I turned. She was a plump woman who wore so much makeup that her face looked like a mask. She stood, feet apart, hands on hips, her thickly penciled eyebrows raised at the sight of me. "Oh," she said, "you're someone else."

"I'm looking for Mr. Adair."

"You ought to be able to tell he isn't home. You people don't give up easy, do you?"

"People?"

"You and the guy who was here before. Although I got to admit you're a better class of visitor."

"There was someone else here? What did he look like?"

"A bum, that's what. In a raincoat and a floppy old hat. Looked like he ought to be hanging out at Wino Park. He kicked the door." She motioned at the gouges. "See?"

"I see. Did you talk with him?"

"Sure I talked with him. What do you think I'd do, with him kicking the door and yelling? I told him it wouldn't do no good. Monty's gone to his country place, left early this morning like he always does."

Adair *must* be getting ahead in the world, if he had a country place. "Where is the place? Near here?"

She shrugged. "Who knows?"

"What did the bum do when you told him Mr. Adair wasn't home?"

"Growled at me. But he left. I tell you, when people like that start coming into the nice neighborhoods! And me, needing my mornings quiet. I mean, I got to be downtown at the department store pushing cosmetics at one, and the morning's the only time I got—"

"Does Mr. Adair go away to the country every week?"

"Huh?"

"You said he went away like he always does."

"Oh, yeah. Tuesday through Friday, regular as clockwork. Then he's back here on the weekends. He's a dealer in art goods, and that's when he does most of his business."

"Art goods, huh?" I smiled faintly. "Well, I guess I'll have to catch him on Friday." I went over and pressed the elevator button.

"Hey," she said, "do you know who that bum was?"

"Do I look like I would know any bums?"

She eyed me critically, frowning so hard I feared for her makeup job. "Nowadays you can't tell." Then she went inside and slammed her door.

I went to my office at All Souls and called the Oasis Bar and Grill. When I asked whether Willie had picked up my message, the man on the other end of the line sounded wary. There were no messages waiting, he said, so Willie must have called in. I left a second one, repeating the first, then hung up and buzzed Hank on the intercom. He said he had talked to Greg Marcus about the murders and would come to my office.

In a minute, he entered, ducking his head to avoid the sharply slanting ceiling, and sat down in my tattered old armchair. He looked tired, rumpled, out of sorts. "You heard from Willie?" he asked.

"Not since his message last night. I've heard *of* him, though. Our paths keep crossing."

"What in hell is he doing?"

"Playing detective."

"Christ! What does he think we have you for?"

"Willie doesn't strike me as the type to sit back and do nothing, particularly if he thinks he'd be doing that in jail."

Hank merely sighed.

"Tell me what Greg had to say. I assume you talked to him because you couldn't get through to McFate."

"Right. I'm afraid you don't have a lead; the Levin murder weapon was something called an RG-14."

"Doesn't matter—now. What else?"

"Alida Edwards was stabbed twice in the neck. There was very little sign of a struggle. The stabbing was quick and efficient, as Greg put it; the killer knew what he was doing."

"What time did she die?"

"Within an hour of when she was found. They were able to establish it by body temperature."

"Who found her? I've assumed it was a passerby."

"Right, a guy from one of those nearby apartment houses who likes to park his car over by Kezar."

"Hmm." I paused. "Hank—do they really think Willie followed her down there and killed her?"

"They want to. Two killings, two nights. It fits."

"It's too pat."

"Cops like pat situations. Besides, there's another detail on the Levin case that makes it look bad for Willie: There was no sign of forced entry at his house."

"Then Levin must have had a key."

"Or have been let in by someone else who did."

"No." I thought of Selena's story of her meeting with Levin. "I think he managed to get hold of a key."

"How? Willie told me he's very careful about his keys. Alida didn't even have one."

"I don't know, but I'll try to find out."

Hank stood up. "I'm due in court in an hour. Try to check with me later."

"Okay." I swiveled my chair around, propped my feet on the armchair, and sat staring at the wall. It was painted pale yellow and was full of thumbtack holes from my various attempts at decoration. When the travel poster of Greece I'd hung there last September had gotten torn and curled at the edges, I'd finally resigned myself to the fact that the office was too small and cheerless to bother sprucing up. Actually, it looked better unadorned.

Suppose, I told myself, Selena *had* copied Willie's keys for Levin. She was a liar; there was no reason to believe she hadn't. But how could she have gotten hold of them? At the flea market, of course. And I remembered seeing a key duplicating stand there.

I got out the phone book and looked up Mack Marchetti's number. He answered on the first ring. "Sharon," he said when I'd identified myself, "I was just on my way out."

"This will only take a second. How can I reach the vendor who duplicates keys at the Saltflats?"

"Bill? He works at the Stonestown shopping center during the week."

"Thanks."

"While I've got you on the line—Selena told me you're a detective. I don't care for being fooled that way."

"I'm sorry. I didn't want to go into it at the time; I needed to locate Willie in a hurry."

"I take it you haven't."

"No, but not for lack of trying. Thanks for the information, Mr. Marchetti." Quickly I depressed the receiver button and looked up the Stonestown Key Shop in the phone book. The man who answered my call said his name was Bill and yes, he was the person who worked at the Saltflats on the weekends. Yes, he knew Selena Gonzalez. No, she had not duplicated any keys within the past two weeks. None of the flea market vendors had, as far as he could remember. In fact, business out there had been lousy and they were thinking of closing the stand.

I hung up and leaned back in my chair, once more at a dead end.

Keys. Willie's house keys. Where did he keep them? On a chain, like I did with mine? A chain with other keys, such as car keys. In Willie's case, truck keys.

I closed my eyes, blotting out the yellow wall, and pictured a scene from Sunday. Willie, handing someone his keys and asking him to get something out of the truck. Willie, saying something about receipts being in the glove compartment.

"Take them in case you need them," he'd said. And then he'd handed the keys to Roger Beck.

I sat up straight and reached for the phone. Would Marchetti know if there was a key duplicating stand at the San Jose market? It was worth a try. I called his number, but there was no answer. Of course, he'd said he was just on his way out.

But hadn't Willie said the San Jose market had an office that was open all week? I called Information, got the number, dialed again. Yes, the woman in the office told me, there was a key stand at the market, and the man who ran it owned a key shop in downtown San Jose. But he was on vacation this week, and the shop was closed.

"Was he also on vacation last Sunday?" I asked.

"No, he was here. But he left yesterday for three weeks' fishing in Idaho, like he does every year."

"Well, thanks anyway." I sat drumming my fingers on the desk blotter, then pulled the notebook where I'd scribbled Beck's phone number and address out of my purse. I called Oakland and talked to a woman who said she was Beck's landlady. Roger was at work, delivering bread for the Crescent Bakery; he was usually back home by three.

I looked at my watch. It was already one-thirty. After Beck finished his delivery route he would have to return the truck to the bakery and complete whatever procedures were required of the drivers. Crescent Bakery was a large plant in West Oakland, visible and easily accessible from Highway 17; if I left now I might be able to catch him there.

chapter eighteen

I grabbed a sandwich in All Souls' kitchen—making do with the end pieces of a loaf of whole wheat bread and some highly suspect tuna salad—and then headed for Oakland. Traffic moved at a crawl over the Bay Bridge, with one lane blocked for repair work. It was the time of day when the semis that had made San Francisco deliveries from ships at the Port of Oakland were returning to the East Bay. They clogged the bridge, jockeying in and out between passenger cars, and giving off great blasts of diesel smoke. The fumes combined with the heat to make me faintly nauseous, and my sinuses began to throb. To keep my mind off my head and stomach, I tried to concentrate on how to approach Roger Beck.

Beck actively hated Willie. Even on Sunday, when I hadn't known the story of Beck and Willie's ex-wife, I had been able to tell that much. If he assumed I was not on Willie's side, he might tell me much more than he would if he thought I was out to help his weekend employer. He might even slip and tell me something really valuable. Besides, I had to face it—there was no way I was going to force a two-hundred-and-fifty-pound truck driver to tell me anything he didn't want to.

The Crescent Bakery occupied a square block between a big warehousing operation and a furniture factory. A dozen of their white trucks with the familiar crescent-shaped roll on the side were parked within a fenced-in area by the loading docks. I pulled up at the curb and watched as more and more of the trucks drove in. They backed up to the docks, where workers off-loaded the plastic racks that had held bread and rolls, then moved to permanent parking spaces. The white-uniformed drivers emerged with clipboards and went into what looked like an office. It was after two-thirty when I saw Beck's burly form ambling across the lot.

After a few minutes I got out of my car and started over there. Several of the drivers were standing around, smoking and talking, and they looked at me curiously. I sat down on the bottom of the steps of the office, and they looked away, obviously assuming I was someone's wife or girlfriend, here to pick him up. When Beck came out and started down the steps, I stood up.

"Mr. Beck," I said.

He looked at me blankly for a moment, then surprise spread across his puffy features. "You're Willie's new runner, aren't you?"

"Yes. Sharon McCone." I reached into my purse and took out the photostat of my license. "Actually, Mr. Beck, I misrepresented myself the other day—both to you and to Mr. Whelan." I held out the photostat.

"A private detective?" He glanced anxiously around at his co-workers.

"Yes. Is there some place we can talk?"

"Is this about Willie?"

"Yes, it is."

"I don't know anything about him. I haven't seen him since Sunday night when I met him at the Oasis and we split the take from the market."

"I didn't expect you had. What I need from you is background information on Mr. Whelan. You could be a big help to me."

"Help you how?"

"Complete my investigation of him."

Beck hesitated. His eyes, sunk deep in his fleshy face, were thoughtful. "You say Willie didn't know you're a detective either?"

"I operate under cover most of the time."

"Why are you checking up on him?"

"Well, Mr. Beck—look at the nature of his business. And now he's evidently killed two people."

Still he paused. "Who are you working for?"

"I'm cooperating with the San Francisco Police Department. Inspector Leo McFate is in charge of the case."

He nodded, seeming reassured by my naming names.

"Is there somewhere we can talk?" I asked again.

"You got a car?"

"Yes."

"You could give me a ride home. Mine's in the shop. I was going to get a lift from one of the other guys, but you could save him the trouble."

"Sure. It's this way." I led him across the lot to the street. We got in the MG and Beck directed me toward the Lake Merritt area of Oakland.

"What I'm interested in," I told him as I drove, "is Mr. Whelan's relationships with his runners. I know there's bad blood between you two—"

"Who told you that?"

"Mr. Whelan."

"He told you about Barbara?"

"His . . . I mean, your ex-wife? Yes."

"Thinks it's pretty funny, does he?"

"Yes, I guess he does."

"You'd think he'd have some sympathy, wouldn't you? I mean, she walked out on him first. He ought to know what it's like, to have a woman like that use you and then leave you and take everything you have. But no, he thinks it's funny. What do you want to know about Willie and his runners?"

I had him where I wanted him. Now I would have to go very carefully. "Well, let's start with Sam Thomas. What's the relationship there?"

"Friends, I guess. Do you know Sam?"

"Yes."

"Then you know he's a drunk. Willie makes excuses for him, calls him a war casualty. Hell, lots of us were over there in 'Nam and we didn't come home and stay plastered day in and day out. But Willie feels sorry for Sam and puts up with some of the damnedest shit. So they *must* be friends."

"What kinds of things does Willie put up with?"

"Oh, like Sam not showing for work. You know, the shit that would get you fired from any regular job."

"I see. What about Monty Adair? Are he and Willie friends?"

"Hell, no. Monty's too slick for Willie; Willie doesn't trust him any farther than he can throw him. I'll say this for Willie, though, he gives credit where credit is due. He always says Monty's the best man he's got."

"How do you feel about him saying that?"

"Doesn't bother me. I'm okay at the job, but I'm no Monty. And for me it's only a weekend job to clean up the bills Barbara stuck me with."

"But you worked for Willie before you married Barbara, didn't you?"

"Oh, yeah. I met her because I was working for Willie. When I first took the job it was so I could buy a boat. But then I fell for Barbara and the money all went for cars and clothes and furniture. All bought on time, and still not paid off." Beck looked away, out the window at the grimy buildings along Grand Avenue.

"How come Willie kept you on, after you took his wife away from him?"

"That's his way of doing things. It saved his pride, made it look like she didn't matter to him."

"Maybe she didn't."

"Maybe."

"To get back to Monty, how would you say he feels about Willie?"

"About the same as most of the people on the flea market scene."

"And how's that?"

"Well, they respect him. He's a sharp trader, knows how to deal. But he's never fit in and he doesn't have any friends."

Except Alida Edwards, I thought.

"No," Beck went on, "Willie was never a friend to any of us, not the way the rest of us were friends, back in the old days."

"The rest of you?"

"Monty, Mack, myself. We used to have real good times."

"Doing what?"

"Drinking beer, chasing women, playing games."

I looked over at him. He was smiling reminiscently. "What kinds of games?"

"We'd shoot some pool, go fishing, play war."

"War?"

"Yeah. Like go out in the country and play the National Survival Game."

I'd seen something about the National Survival Game in the paper recently. "You mean where adults play capture-the-flag with toy guns?"

Beck frowned. "It's not that simple. I mean, it's a real sport, with a manual and all. There's a national organization, and they have playing fields in most of the states, Canada too. And the guns aren't toys."

Now I frowned. "They're not?"

"No. You turn right here."

I did as he directed, driving along the boulevard that bordered Lake Merritt. "What are they then? You don't use real bullets, do you?"

"Of course not. They're paint guns, shoot pellets the size of marbles, full of yellow paint. When you're hit, you yell 'paint check,' and one of the officials comes up and makes sure it's a legal hit."

Paint. I remembered the gun in Mack Marchetti's living room display case, the one he'd said was for marking stock on ranches. I'd been about to ask him why he had one when the phone had rung and Selena had told him about Alida's murder.

"And if it's a legal hit?" I said.

"You're out of the game, same as if you're dead."

"Oh." The concept of grown men running around and shooting one another with paint was faintly ridiculous. "What's the object of all this?"

"To capture the other team's flag. They give you a battle map, showing where it's at, and whichever side gets to the other's flag first wins."

"It sounds like cowboys and Indians to me."

Beck rolled his eyes. "Women never understand these things."

"Explain it to me, then."

"The game is a good release for tensions. The way the world is today, you need that. Take me: This morning I go in and they load up the truck. They short me on one order. The guy at the restaurant where I'm delivering yells at me, like I loaded the truck personally. Christ, he acted like I'd *baked* the stuff! Can I yell back at him, though? No. He's the customer; the customer's always right.

"So I go back to the bakery. I complain about being shorted. The shift boss doesn't listen. Can I yell at him for not listening? Not if I want to keep my job. Can I yell at the guy who shorted me? I don't even know who did it, and anyway he's gone for the day. So what do I have? Tension. What can I do about it? Nothing."

"So what you're saying is that the Survival Game is good therapy."

"Yeah. You're out there, you got your gun, you're equal to any of the other players. You can do something about things for a change. You're somebody, you've got power."

"Does it cost a lot to play?"

"Maybe forty bucks. There's an entry fee, and you've got to rent your fatigues and goggles and gun. Some guys, like Mack, cut the cost by owning their own gear—but it's got to be regulation."

"Does anyone else from the flea markets besides you and Mack play the game?"

"Sure. Monty, about five, six of the other vendors. Even some women played."

"Selena Gonzalez?"

"Nah, not that I know of."

"What about Alida?"

"Hell, no."

"And not Willie?"

"Never Willie. It used to piss him off that we played, because we'd take a weekend off from the markets to do it."

"Where do you play?"

"Like I said, there are places in practically every state. We used to go to one in Contra Costa County, near Mount Diablo. You need a lot of room, and it's got to be kind of rough country for it to be any fun."

"I've never noticed any of these places."

"Well, they don't exactly stick up a sign. While it's just a game, it's not a spectator sport. I mean, somebody could get hurt if they got in the players' way."

"So how do you find out where to play?"

"There's a directory you can buy. You better turn right here."

I signaled and started up the hill, which was honeycombed with old stucco apartments and rooming houses. "So you and Monty and Mack play at this place in Contra Costa County."

"I do; they don't anymore."

"Why not?"

He shrugged, uncomfortable. "A couple of years ago they found some place else closer to home."

"Where?"

"I'm not sure. That's my driveway there."

The house was two stories, green stucco with a red tile roof. Its small yard was unkempt and the hydrangeas in the flower beds were browning and badly in need of water. A sign in the front window advertised ROOMS TO LET. I turned in and stopped. "Why didn't you start playing at the new place with them?"

He shrugged again. "They wanted a rougher game, something more challenging. I wasn't up for that. Besides, I didn't like who they were playing with."

"Who was it?"

"That Jew-boy who got himself shot in Willie's garage. I couldn't take him, and it's not because I'm prejudiced against Jews either. I mean, I got plenty of Jewish friends. I'm not prejudiced at all—not like Mack and Monty."

It surprised me so much that I let out the clutch and stalled the car. "Jerry Levin, is that who you mean?"

"Yeah. Jerry was Monty and Mack's big buddy for a while there. I couldn't stand him myself."

"Why?"

"Because he was one vicious little motherfucker. I mean, when he played those games, it was like he was playing for real. I got the feeling he liked to see people get hurt." He paused, his hand on the door handle. "Funny."

"What's funny?"

"Well, Mack and Monty are a couple of the most prejudiced guys I know. I mean, they hated Jerry Levin and only hung around him because he had money. But now that I think back on Levin, I realize he was even more bigoted than them. He hated everybody, no matter what their race or religion was. Hell, he even hated his own people."

"Wait a minute—you say Levin had money?"

"That's what I gathered from what Mack and Monty told me. You see, they wanted to open their own game, break away from the national organization and form a new one that would play a tougher, harder game. I think Levin either had the money to do it, or else knew how to get it."

I stared at Beck, stunned. Of course. Jerry Levin may not have had the money, but he *did* know how to get his hands on it. How it must have amused a trio of bigots like Marchetti, Adair, and Levin to finance what was basically a right-wing sport with the proceeds from Torahs stolen from Jewish congregations.

chapter nineteen

Before I let Beck get out of the car, I remembered to ask him if he'd duplicated any keys at the flea market recently. He looked genuinely puzzled and said he certainly hadn't. I believed him; there was no reason Beck would put himself out for Jerry Levin, who had intruded on his formerly good-natured beer-buddy friendship with Marchetti and Adair. I left him standing next to a wilted hydrangea bush in his front yard, looking confused at my abrupt question and even more abrupt departure.

I drove rapidly toward San Francisco and All Souls, glad the rush-hour traffic was headed the other way. Details of the case were whirling around in my mind. I still had the problem of how Levin got into Willie's house. And add to that the image of grown men playing a lunatic sport in the hills of Contra Costa County. Grown men shooting at each other with yellow paint pellets. . . .

All Souls was quiet when I got there, and Ted sat at the reception desk doing one of his ever-present crossword puzzles.

"Five-letter word that's a prefix for 'backward,'" he called as I passed him.

"'Retro,'" I said and kept going toward Hank's office. I myself was not bad at puzzles.

Hank sat at his desk, feet propped on a bottom drawer, a brief in one hand. He looked up as I came in, then took off his glasses and rubbed his eyes. "Any news?"

"Some, but I haven't figured out what it means yet. Can I use your phone?"

He motioned toward it. I picked up the receiver and called the Oasis Bar and Grill. The background noise was overpowering; business must be good on this Tuesday evening. I asked if Willie had picked up my message. He had, the man said. I left the same one, knowing all the while that the fence would disregard it in the way he had my others.

Then I phoned my answering service. They had a message *from* Willie. It said, "I'm getting closer."

"Terrific. I wish I was." I slammed the receiver down and went over to Hank's stack of the San Francisco *Chronicle*. It was about three feet high and went back several weeks.

"What are you doing?" Hank asked, putting his glasses back on.

"Looking for an article on the National Survival Game."

"Try April, around the thirteenth."

"Thanks." It didn't even surprise me anymore when he did that. Hank was a media junkie and had a copious memory for dates and figures. I was pulling the right issue out of the stack—it was the fifteenth; he'd only been off by two days—when the intercom buzzed. Hank answered it, then held the receiver out to me. "Call for you."

It was Rabbi David Halpert. "Was the information I gave your associate all right?" he asked.

"What information?"

"About what you and Ben Cohen and I discussed yesterday."

"What associate?"

"A Hank Zahn. He said he was working with you and wanted to check some details. We went over the whole conversation, and he said he'd get back to me with some further questions, but I haven't heard. He also spoke briefly with Ben."

"When was this?"

"Around two o'clock."

I glanced over at Hank, who had gone back to reading the brief. At two o'clock Hank had been in court.

Willie.

"I hope the information agreed with what we talked about," Halpert said anxiously. "He asked a lot of questions, as if he was afraid I'd left something out."

"No, the information was just fine. I asked Mr. . . . Zahn to verify it because sometimes I don't trust my memory."

Hank looked up, curious.

"I saw where there was another killing," Halpert said.

"Yes."

"Are you investigating that one too?"

"In a way. Thanks for giving Mr. Zahn the information, David. I'll let you know how the case turns out." I handed the receiver back to Hank.

"What information am I supposed to have verified for you?" he asked.

"You, in the person of Willie Whelan, got the details on Jerry Levin from Rabbi Halpert."

"You mean Willie impersonated me?"

"I'm willing to bet he did."

"Jesus Christ!" Hank tossed the brief on the desk. "He still thinks he's a detective."

"Yes. And he's going about it in a very logical, methodical manner. Maybe he missed his calling." Then I sat down and started reading the article on the National Survival Game. Hank got up and left the office. I suspected he was going down the hill to his favorite sleazy bar—the Remedy Lounge—for a shot or two of Scotch.

The article confirmed what Roger Beck had told me. The game was the brainchild of some East Coast types who had later quit their jobs and incorporated, selling franchises all over the country. Around ten thousand people played it weekly in the United States and Canada. There was an official manual and national championships. Experts had various opinions on it, ranging from benign attitudes of indulgence to outright alarm. One man had likened it to a "real live video game." And, like the manufacturers of video games, people were getting rich off the survival game, selling everything from military fatigues to paint guns.

I seemed to be hearing a lot about guns these days. There was the .22 that had killed Levin . . . Selena's "plinker," now in the possession of Willie . . . Mack Marchetti's Nel-Spot 007 . . . Fat Herman's sinister stock . . . Monty Adair's frequent visits to the gun shop . . . Herman, saying, "I'm not one of the Krupp family . . ."

I jumped up and went down the hall to the reception area. Ted looked up and said, "Six-letter word meaning—"

"Never mind. Listen, you pick up a lot of trivia through those puzzles, right?"

"Yeah."

"Tell me about the Krupp Arms Works."

"That's not trivia. That's big stuff."

"Big weapons, right?"

"Yeah."

"Supplied most of the German arms during World War II?"

"Yeah, and—"

"Mainly military arms, huh?"

"Yes. They—"

"Thanks." I started for the door.

"Hey, I thought you wanted *me* to tell *you* about Krupp."

I didn't answer him; I was already on the front steps.

Selena Gonzalez was at home, but she didn't want to let me in. After she yelled for me to go away, I kept pounding on her door.

"I said, go away!"

"No. I have to talk with you."

"Leave me alone!"

"Let me in."

"You will disturb my neighbors."

"Then open the door."

Finally she did. Casting a sullen look at me, she went and sat on the floor amid a litter of plastic sandwich bags. Big tubs that contained dried fruit and nuts were lined up in front of her.

"Getting ready for the flea market next weekend?" I asked.

"Yes. They bring the food from the plant where I buy it on Tuesday. I spend the rest of my week putting it in the bags and pasting my label on the jars." She motioned at several cases of olives that sat on the kitchen counter.

"Looks like a hard week's work."

She didn't catch the irony in my voice. "Work is what you make it."

I sat down crosslegged behind a tub of dried banana chips and viewed her over it. She looked even worse than the night before; her face was pale and puffy and her hair straggled from combs that seemed to have been stuck into it at random. When she saw me studying her, she picked up a bag and began filling it with corn nuts.

"Selena," I said, "when I was here last night you told me you met Jerry Levin when he bought some fruit from you."

She hesitated, then continued filling the bag. "That is true."

"No, it's not. I want to know how you really met him—and when."

"He bought some fruit from me—"

"No, Selena."

She reached for a stapler that sat beside her, picked up a label, and sealed the bag, stapling the label to it at the same time.

"You've known Levin for a long time, haven't you? Ever since he and Mack Marchetti and Monty Adair used to play those war games."

She was silent, tossing the bag on a pile of full ones and reaching for another to fill.

"Where did you meet Levin?"

She looked up, eyes flashing with about a third of their former spark. "All right! I met him at Mack's house. Once. And that is all. Is it a crime to meet someone at a friend's house?"

"No, not if it had stopped there. But you met Levin again, at

David's, the day Sam Thomas saw you. Why did you go there?"

"To have lunch! Why does anyone go to a delicatessen?"

"No, Selena, you had more on your mind than bagels and lox."

She began putting corn nuts in the bag.

"Last night you also said that Jerry Levin wanted keys to Willie's house so he could retrieve the Torahs. I know he got those keys. From you."

Her hand faltered and corn nuts rolled onto the floor.

"What I wonder," I added, "is how you duplicated them."

"I didn't!"

"Then who did?"

"Monty. Monty did."

Of course. If Willie occasionally gave Beck his keys and asked him to get things from the truck, he could just as easily have given them to Adair. "When?"

"I don't know. He dropped them off here on Saturday night."

Possibly he'd duplicated them that day, or even the week before, after Selena had reported Levin wanted them. "And when did you give them to Levin?"

"After the flea market on Sunday. We met in the parking lot. Monty told me to tell Levin that Willie was never home from five to seven on Sunday evenings."

That was the time for which he had refused to give himself an alibi. "Where does he go then?"

"I do not know."

"Did Monty say why he wanted Levin to have the keys?"

"No. I guess he wanted him to have his Torahs."

That made no sense at all. "Are you sure he didn't explain it to you?"

"They never tell me anything."

They. "Selena, last night you also said that people are always making you do things you don't want to, by threatening to turn you in to Immigration."

"That is true. I am in a very delicate position."

"Is that why you gave the keys to Levin? Because Monty threatened you?"

She was silent, staring down at the spilled corn nuts.

"Did he also make you meet with Levin that day at David's?"

Again, silence.

"Selena!"

"They wanted to know what Jerry Levin was thinking. They had

had some business, and then there had been a falling out."

"What kind of business?"

"They did not tell me."

"What caused the falling out?"

"I think that happened when Jerry Levin rediscovered his faith. They wanted to know how serious he was about it, and why he was always at the flea market, watching."

"So you talked to him and found out?"

"Yes. They made me."

"By 'they,' you mean Monty Adair and Mack Marchetti?"

She nodded.

"What's your relationship with Marchetti?"

"What do you mean?"

"Well, you called him right away when you heard Alida was dead. And you must have talked to him today because I spoke with him earlier and he said you'd told him I was a detective."

"Oh."

"Does he make you do a lot of things, in exchange for not turning you in to Immigration?"

She spread out her hands, palms up, and waved them wearily. "Oh, not so many things. I see him, that is all."

" 'See' him?"

"Yes. You know."

I'd suspected as much. "You must really hate Mexico."

"One does what one has to. I am alone in this country; I need a protector."

"But for a man to force you—"

"He is a man. He does not know any better. Besides," she added with a trace of her former sparkle, "I hate Mexico far more than I hate Mack Marchetti."

I had no answer for that. And since I had found out what I'd come here for, I left her alone amid her plastic bags and banana chips and corn nuts.

chapter twenty

I had a fairly good idea now of the way things had happened and why, but it still wasn't enough to pin the crimes on anyone or to clear Willie. And that was my primary responsibility, wasn't it— to clear my client? I drove home, turning the facts over in my mind, trying to make concrete connections.

The house looked lonely and abandoned in the dusky light. Don wasn't there, nor was there any note or other indication he'd returned after his lunch with his friend at KSUN. It was just as well, I told myself. I had too much on my mind right now to deal with personal problems. Still, the place was mighty cheerless, and even Watney rubbing around my legs failed to lift my gloom. I picked him up and sat down on the couch in the living room to think about Monty Adair.

The sharp-eyed flea market vendor had been calm and collected when I'd gone to his apartment last night. How long was that after Alida had been killed? An hour? Two?

Of course, I hadn't said anything about the murder to Adair. All I'd said was that I wanted to locate Willie. And it had been too early for the story to be on the news; Selena hadn't heard it until ten, and she had probably had her radio on all evening. So, as far as Adair was concerned, there was no cause to be nervous when I arrived. He might have assumed the body wouldn't be discovered until morning. And with any luck on his part, it might not have been.

But instead, she had been found, and the police and news reporters had come. . . .

I looked over at my stereo setup and the tape deck with which Don had been recording KSUN's prime-time show the night before. The tape was still advanced to where it had run out. I set Watney down on the couch and went over to the stereo, turning on the power switch and then rewinding the tape about halfway. I punched the play button, listened to the tail end of a particularly horrible New Wave selection, and then heard the d.j.'s voice announce the time as nine-fifteen. I pushed the fast forward button, played some more, and repeated the procedure several times until I found the ten o'clock news broadcast.

". . . And in the local news, the body of a young woman, Alida Edwards of San Francisco, was found stabbed to death in the shrubbery near Kezar Stadium earlier this evening. Ms. Edwards was a jewelry designer and member of a prominent Houston, Texas, family. Police have issued an all-points bulletin for Ms. Edwards' fiancé, William Whelan, of San Francisco. . . ."

I pressed the stop button, stood there for a moment, then started to rewind the tape so I could listen to the news broadcast again. The phone rang, and I glanced at it in irritation. The calls should be transferring over to the service, but after four rings I realized they weren't. Don must have returned at some point during the day, used the phone, and forgotten to switch it back—and that, plus the lack of a note from him, was a bad sign.

I turned the tape deck off, crossed the room, and answered the phone. There was a lot of noise on the line, background noise like you'd hear if the call came from a bar. I could barely hear what the caller was saying.

"Sharon? It's Willie."

"Willie! It's about time. Where the hell are you?"

His reply was muffled.

"What?"

"Can't talk now. Can you meet me at the Oasis? In twenty minutes. There's a little alley behind, go there. Don't go inside."

"Willie, what have you—"

"Twenty minutes." He hung up.

I glared at the receiver and slammed it down. I'd better get going or I wouldn't make it on time and then Willie might not wait. I needed to get my hands on him, tell him what I'd found out, and then convince him to turn himself in to the police. When he did that, I'd tell them everything I knew. They could take it from there, but I wasn't giving them anything until Hank was around to protect Willie.

I grabbed my purse, pulled a heavy sweater from the bedroom closet, and had just started toward the front door when the bell rang. I kept going, jerked the door open, and came face-to-face with Inspector Leo McFate.

"Dammit!" I said.

McFate raised one eyebrow politely. "Is something wrong, Ms. McCone?"

"I was just on my way out. I . . . I have a date."

"A date." He looked quizzically at my Irish knit sweater, jeans, and tennis shoes, as if he couldn't believe a person would go out of the house dressed this way, let alone on a date.

"Yes," I said firmly. "What can I do for you?"

He glanced around the front porch, an obvious hint that I should ask him in. I remained in the doorway. Finally he said, "I was in the neighborhood and thought I'd stop by to check some of the details in your statement on the Levin murder."

"Can't this wait until tomorrow?"

"Ms. McCone, this is a homicide investigation. Surely you know we don't keep regular hours when we're on a case."

"All right. What do you want to know?"

I expected him to take out a notepad, but he didn't. McFate, I now recalled, was reputed to have a photographic memory and prided himself on it. "You stated that you and Mr. Whelan arrived at his house at eight o'clock that evening."

"Approximately." I glanced at my watch. If I didn't get to the Oasis quickly, Willie might not wait.

"Approximately. And you found the body when?"

"Eight-ten."

"When you entered the house, which one of you noticed it had been ransacked?"

"Well, we both noticed. It was obvious—"

"Did you or Mr. Whelan first call attention to the fact something was wrong there?"

I shifted impatiently from foot to foot. "He noticed the door to the garage was open. And then he went into the living room, turned on the light, and we both saw—"

"So it was *Mr. Whelan* who called attention to the ransacking."

"I guess you could say that."

"You guess."

"Yes, it was Mr. Whelan."

"Good. Now, Ms. McCone, you stated that you were the first to go down to the garage."

"Yes. Willie . . . Mr. Whelan was right behind me."

"And you were the first to notice Mr. Levin's body."

"Yes, but again Willie was right there and noticed it almost at the same time."

"But you first called attention to it."

"Yes."

"Did it ever occur to you that Mr. Whelan was *letting* you find the body first?"

"What does that mean? You think he killed Levin, ransacked his own house, and then let me discover it?"

"It's possible."

"It may be possible, but that's not what happened."

"How do you know that?"

I hesitated.

"Well?"

"Inspector, are you finished with your questions? Because if you are, I really do have to go."

"Ah, yes. Your date. It wouldn't be with Mr. Whelan, by any chance?"

Was it just a shot, or did he know something? "With Willie? You've got to be joking."

"I understand you've been pursuing this investigation, talking to people who know him."

"Of course I'm pursuing it; I work for his attorney; we have to build a defense."

"I only hope you're pursuing it in a legal and ethical way. I've heard things about you, Ms. McCone."

"Such as?"

"I've heard that sometimes you conduct your investigations in a manner that could be termed obstructive."

I glared at him, my hand tightening on the doorknob. "Have I ever been charged with obstruction? Have I ever been brought up before the licensing board?"

"Not yet." He studied my face thoughtfully. "Perhaps I could help you give a more positive direction to your career."

"In what way?"

"Perhaps we could get together some time and talk about proper procedure, how you can help rather than hinder the department. Nothing formal, you understand, just conversation over drinks or dinner."

It was a pass. And a backhanded, snotty sort of pass, at that. I stared at him.

He turned and started down the steps. "I'll give you a call in a few days, set something up."

I stood there, speechless, and then I noticed a hammer that was lying on the porch next to the pot of geraniums. For a moment I had a violent urge to pick it up and whack McFate on the head with it. Fortunately, I contented myself with slamming the door.

Now I was really late for my appointment with Willie. He'd told me to go to the alley behind the bar rather than inside, but that didn't mean he wouldn't go in, perhaps to check for messages. I hurried down the hall and called the Oasis. I asked the bartender to tell Willie, if he came in, that I still intended to meet him. "Please tell him to wait," I said. "Tell him I'll be there soon."

I slammed down the receiver, looked out the front window to see if McFate was gone, and then ran outside to my MG.

The fog was in on the west side of the hill near the Medical Center, but it was not nearly so thick as on the previous night. I drove toward Irving Street, thinking over what I knew.

Monty Adair, Mack Marchetti, Roger Beck, and God knew how many other denizens of the flea market world had been accustomed to playing weekend soldier at a National Survival Game franchise somewhere in Contra Costa County. For Adair and Marchetti, as well as their unlikely friend Jerry Levin, the game hadn't been enough. They had told Roger Beck they planned to open their own game site, playing a "rougher and more challenging" version.

I thought I knew what "rougher and more challenging" meant.

First, of course, they needed a method of financing the project. Adair was doing all right as one of Willie's runners, but he probably spent every cent of it on such front as the Pacific Heights studio. Marchetti made a decent living from running the Saltflats, mainly because he permitted so much illegal dealing there, but still it wouldn't have been enough. The game—or their new version of it—required a large tract of land, and land was expensive in Northern California. Thus, they needed a way to raise a great deal of money.

Enter Jerry Levin and his stolen Torahs. Perhaps the scheme was developed solely for the purpose of financing their project; the timing fit. Either way, Levin had become their fund-raiser.

What then? They had purchased land, and I had a good idea where. Jerry Levin owned that cabin in the Santa Cruz Mountains, and he would doubtless know of available sites. I was fairly certain their new playing field was down in the valley that bordered on Levin's mountain acreage. After all, there was evidence someone had been playing war there, shooting off the Nel-Spot 007. I'd seen the yellow paint streaks on the trees, but at the time had chalked it up to something to do with the fire, perhaps a flame retardant. Also, if that were the site of their new land, it would explain why I'd been shot at. They wouldn't want strangers snooping around there.

But why had anyone been firing the paint-pellet gun there? Had their whole scheme really started as a variant of the National Survival Game? Or did they train with the Nel-Spot because it was quiet and cheaper to use than a real weapon? It didn't matter; what did was the fact that their game had quickly turned into something far more serious and deadly than playing war.

"I'm not a member of the Krupp family."

That was what Fat Herman had said when he'd spoken of Adair's interest in buying weapons from him. Herman would go outside the law and sell untraceable guns under the counter, but he didn't supply big guns—machine guns, mortars, the sort of weapon a paramilitary encampment would require.

I pulled into a parking lot a block away from the Oasis, parked the car, and took a shortcut through a pizza restaurant, still pondering.

Had the group gotten their hands on those kinds of weapons? The gun that had been fired at me when I'd been exploring Levin's former land had probably been an ordinary hunting rifle. What Herman had been alluding to was more firepower than that.

And what had happened with Jerry Levin and the Torahs? He'd rediscovered his religion, Selena had maintained. Maybe it was a genuine religious conversion. If so, he would have reason to hold back the Torahs from the others. But that made no sense; if Levin could have gotten them *into* Willie's garage and stashed them with the player piano rolls, he could also have gotten them *out*. There would have been no need for him to watch Willie and ask Selena to get him keys to the house.

Okay, forget that for a minute. Levin got religion. What then? His enemies—meaning the others in the organization—tried to destroy him. How? By burning his cabin? Probably. After all, Jack Foxx, the Arson Squad inspector, had said the site had the signs of a deliberately set blaze. Why hadn't Levin gone to the authorities, then? Possibly he couldn't prove who had done it, and also didn't want to incriminate himself.

And then Levin came to San Francisco, determined to rescue his Torahs. And had been given keys to Willie's house by Selena. I hadn't thought to ask her, but it was obvious that Adair had made not one but two sets of keys. Levin had used one—and died. And then, since the keys hadn't been found on his body, the killer had removed them.

I thought I knew who that killer was, too. But there were loose ends. Too many loose ends. . . .

The alley that ran behind the Oasis opened up onto one of the sidestreets. I rounded the corner and started down there, peering through the darkness for Willie. There were cars pulled up on either side, their wheels on the sidewalks, almost flush against the buildings so other vehicles could pass. I didn't see the borrowed van, but that didn't surprise me. Willie would probably approach on foot, as unobtrusively as possible. I spied the floodlit sign indicating the rear entrance to the bar. No one waited there.

Of course, I thought, Willie would be in disguise, probably wearing his derelict outfit. And he certainly wouldn't stand out in the open where a passing patrol car might spot him. I went as far as the entrance to the bar and looked up and down the alley again. No sign of anyone.

Damn McFate! If he had only come to my house a few minutes later, I would have already been on my way to this appointment. As it was, he had delayed me a good ten minutes and caused me to exercise undue caution, driving here by a circuitous route in case he really suspected my so-called date was with Willie. There was no telling, without going inside, whether Willie had checked the bar for messages when I didn't show on time. But even if he hadn't, he might have gone away, intending to return here later. There was nothing to do but wait.

It was cold there in the alley. I pushed my hands into the pockets of my sweater and began to pace. My watch showed close to eight. Had Willie given me up and gone off on another of his tangents?

I'd better go inside and use the phone to check my answering service. Maybe he'd left another message.

But he had specifically said not to go into the bar.

Still . . .

I started over toward the floodlit sign. There was a sudden rushing noise behind me. Before I could turn, hands gripped me. I tried to wrench away, but they held me tighter. Then an arm hooked around my neck, and a cloth was pressed over my nose and mouth. A rough cloth, damp, reeking of—

I struggled harder, kicked out, tried to dig at him with my elbows. Futile. A chloroform-suffused darkness was closing over me, and there was not a damned thing I could do about it. . . .

chapter twenty-one

My head ached worse than it ever had in my life. Each throb set off flashes of light behind my eyelids. My sinuses were plugged and I felt queasy.

And then came the memory of suffocating chloroform fumes. Chloroform, and strong arms pinning me. The alley behind the Oasis Bar and Grill. Willie . . .

I forced my eyes open to a slit. The light was more blinding than the ones exploding in my brain. I focused on a nubby green material and curving rattan arms. A couch. I was lying on a couch.

Opening my lids further, I looked past the couch to the rest of the room. There was a metal desk and a bank of file cabinets. An office of some kind. Painfully I moved my gaze to the far right, where a man sat on a stool. A man clad in olive drab fatigues, holding a rifle across his lap. Monty Adair.

I shut my eyes, but not fast enough. Adair said, "Ah, Sharon. You're awake."

I tried to speak, but my lips and tongue were cottony dry. I swallowed and tried again. "You were the one. In the alley. Called me pretending to be Willie." My words were thick and slurred.

"Very perceptive of you, considering you've been out cold for a good three hours."

Three hours. That would make it . . . make it around eleven at night. I wanted to ask him where we were, but it seemed too much of an effort. Instead I lay there for a few minutes, letting my head clear. Adair watched me impassively.

Finally I said, "Where am I?"

"Where do you think?"

I wasn't in any shape for guessing games. Raising myself on one elbow, I started to sit up. A wave of nausea forced me down again. I waited for it to pass, then said, "Paramilitary camp."

"That's very good." He nodded as if I'd just passed a difficult examination.

"You brought me here."

"Right again."

"Why?"

"Mack wants to talk to you."

I made it up this time and swung my feet off the couch onto the floor. The nausea came back, then subsided some. "About what?"

"Oh come now, Sharon. You know. You know too much."

"I know you set up your own camp. Did you buy the land?"

"Yes. Levin found it for us."

"It's near his cabin. You burned his cabin."

"Yes."

"Why?" My head was more clear now and the light was not as painful anymore.

"He didn't play fair with us. We should have known better than to deal with a Jew. So we set the place on fire so it would look like an accident, and he went away."

"What was he going to do, give the Torahs back to the congregations he stole them from?"

"Yes."

"Was he really serious about this religious conversion?"

"Entirely serious. It seems he did a lot of thinking up there in the woods."

"So he hid the Torahs in Willie's garage where you couldn't get at them?"

"No. *I* hid them there. Levin was being watched. By those Nazi-hunters, or whatever they claim to be. He was afraid to keep the Torahs with him. So one day when I was picking up some merchandise from Willie, I put them in with the player piano rolls."

"Why didn't you just keep them at your apartment? You weren't being watched."

"I don't keep anything illegal at my apartment. It's too much of a risk. For years now I've used Willie's garage. Hot merchandise, controlled substances, anything like that goes there."

"Does Willie know this?"

"Of course not."

"Weren't you afraid he'd find out?"

"No. That garage is like a pack rat's nest. He can barely find the stuff *he* puts there."

It was a clever practice for a young man getting ahead in the world, I thought.

I sensed I could get the whole story from Adair, if I let him talk. He loved to listen to himself, to lecture and expound. But I was more concerned with what they intended to do with me. I raised my head and looked around the room. It had stone walls and a heavy oak door with massive iron hinges. There were windows, small casement types, but they were covered with thick shutters.

"How many are there in your group?" I asked.

"Enough."

"Enough for what?"

"To protect ourselves, our way of life. We don't like what's happening in this country. Rampant liberalism. Women stepping out of their place. Welfare cheats. Minorities demanding things. We've got to be prepared, and this camp gives us the training we need."

"To do what?"

"I just told you. To protect ourselves, our homes. Our families."

It was scary stuff. Very scary. "Do you train with real weapons?"

"Not yet. For most maneuvers, the type of gun used in the National Survival Game is adequate. We haven't raised the money for our real weapons yet."

"Levin was supposed to do that, with the remaining Torahs."

"Yes. His change of attitude caused us a real problem. I had told him the Torahs were at Willie's. My first mistake. At least I didn't tell him where. But he went to San Francisco after we burned him out. Began watching Willie. We were afraid the Nazi-hunters would realize why."

"So if you didn't want Levin to take the Torahs, why did you have Selena give him the keys to Willie's house?" I glanced at the shutters once again; they were nailed together.

"We thought we could convince him to come back into the fold—temporarily. So he could sell the rest of the Torahs for us."

"But why convince him at Willie's?"

"Because it was the one place we knew he wanted to go. We knew we could lure him to Willie's." Adair shook his head. "I thought it was a bad idea. Look how it turned out."

"Why tear up Willie's house, though, if you knew where the Torahs were?"

Adair looked surprised. "We didn't."

"Someone did, looking for those Torahs. And it wasn't Levin, because the person looked in places where the Torahs wouldn't have fit. Levin knew how large they were."

He shrugged. "I don't know anything about that."

"Had Mack ever seen a Torah?"

Adair's eyes widened and he raised his brows. "How do you figure it was Mack?"

I didn't want to tell him that I knew Marchetti had killed both Levin and Alida. And I certainly wasn't about to explain about the radio tape. About how Marchetti had told me Alida had been stabbed in the neck immediately after Selena had called to tell him about the murder, but before that particular detail had been released to the press. If I told Adair that, I might never get out of here.

"Just a guess," I finally said.

He watched me, eyes narrowed.

"I was wrong about Mack, huh?"

"Yes."

I felt a twinge of relief. If Adair was determined to hide the fact Marchetti had committed the murders, it might still be possible for me to talk my way out of this.

Adair shifted on the stool, steadying the rifle across his lap.

I looked at it, wondering what my chances were of taking it away from him. Nil, I decided. "Was it you that shot at me the other day, when I was up there at Levin's cabin?"

"No. I was in the city."

"Mack, then."

He shrugged again, smiling unpleasantly.

I looked around the room, avoiding his eyes. It was sparsely furnished, with only the file cabinets, desk, and this ratty old couch, which probably had been left here by the previous owners. The group didn't seem to be doing too well financially, as evidenced by their desperation over getting Levin back into the fold so he could sell the remaining Torahs.

"It's been expensive, getting set up here, hasn't it?" I said.

"Yes. The land was high-priced. We had to convert some of the buildings for our use. Make repairs. It's been costly."

Very costly, I thought. Two lives' worth. I shivered.

"My goodness, Sharon, are you all right?" he asked caustically.

I placed my elbows on my knees and lowered my face into my hands. It was a ruse to give me time to think. Perhaps there was some way to deal with these people—

"You women should know better than to force your way into professions you're not suited for," Adair said. "If you'd kept to your place, none of this would be happening."

A retort rose to my lips, but I stifled it. I had an idea now. This kind of man had a certain view of women. It went with his right-wing politics. According to people like Adair or Marchetti, women were weak, pliant, and easily frightened. If I conformed to that image, I would pose less of a threat to them.

"You know, you're not even a very good detective," Adair

added. "You asked all the wrong questions of the wrong people—like asking Mack about the key duplicating service at the Saltflats. And bullying Selena—you didn't think she would keep it from Mack, did you?"

Instead of answering, I clutched my stomach and leaned forward. "Monty, I feel sick."

"The chloroform should have worn off by now."

"But I'm sick! And I'm scared. Please, won't you let me go home—"

The door opened. I looked up and saw Mack Marchetti. He also wore olive drab fatigues, and his bearing was rigidly military. Adair suddenly sat up straighter.

"What's going on here?" Marchetti said. He snapped the words out crisply, an officer speaking to one of his men.

"She claims she's sick."

"Well, she probably is. You kept giving her more chloroform every time she started to come around, all the way down here."

"What else was I supposed to do?" In contrast to Marchetti, Adair looked like a malingering private.

"Nothing," Marchetti said. "I'm just pointing out that there might be a good reason for her to be sick."

There was an abrasive note in Marchetti's voice, and I sensed I had stumbled upon a schism within the paramilitary organization. The two men might not be as solid a team as I'd assumed. That was something I could work on.

"Mr. Marchetti," I said, "I'm awfully sick." I gagged a little for emphasis.

Marchetti sighed. I half expected him to exclaim, "Women!" Instead he turned to Adair and said, "I can't talk to her if she's going to puke."

"It's not the chloroform, I tell you. She's scared."

"Do you blame me?" I put a convincing quaver into my voice. It wasn't hard; I *was* scared.

"Goddamn it," Marchetti said, "what have you been doing to her?"

"Me?" Adair got off the stool. "I haven't done a damn thing—"

"Yeah, like you didn't tell me where those fucking scrolls were—"

"I'm going to throw up!" I clapped a hand to my mouth.

"Oh Jesus!" Marchetti's voice was panicked. "Get her out of here! Get her out, for Christ's sake, until she's calmed down."

"What am I supposed to do with her?"

I made another gagging sound.

"Jesus! Take her . . . take her to that storeroom. If she pukes, there's nothing in there she can hurt. I'll talk to her later."

Adair came over to me and grabbed my arm. "Get up."

I groaned.

"Get up!" He yanked me to my feet and pushed me toward the door.

Adair put the tip of the rifle barrel against my spine and forced me through the door into a dim corridor. I went quietly. The walls here were stone too, interrupted at intervals by reinforced archways that opened into darkness. The air was musty and pungent, like the air in some old wineries I'd visited. I thought of the grape plants I'd seen growing on the hill, and the stone buildings in the valley below the ruins of Levin's cabin. They must have bought a defunct winery. Even though the redwood casks were no longer here, the odor from possibly a hundred years of winemaking lingered.

Adair pushed me along the corridor to another massive wooden door at its end. It was secured with a heavy hasp and padlock. He opened it and motioned me inside. It was pitch dark in there, and cold.

"There's a bucket some place," he said. "If you're going to puke, use that." Then he shut the door and I heard the padlock snap.

I stood still, my eyes adjusting to the dark. Gradually areas of greater and lesser shadow began to stand out. I reached to my right and encountered rough planking. There were things lined up on it that felt like cans.

A storeroom, Marchetti had said. What did they keep in here? I moved over to the shelves and felt along them. Boxes, cans, cloth. I groped my way back to the door and searched on either side of it for a light switch. Nothing.

As I stood there in the dark, I began to feel claustrophobic. I wished I were anywhere else, and thought of home. And the thought of home made me think of Don. Was he there by now? Was he worried about me? How long before he realized something had happened?

Stop this right now, I told myself. Try to find a way out of this mess.

If only I had a light. . . .

There was a small flashlight in my purse, but I had no idea what had happened to the bag. It might still be back in the alley behind the Oasis. I'd give a lot for that flashlight; it was very dark in here, and my eyes had adjusted all they were going to. If I could only find some matches. . . .

I felt in the pocket of my jeans, and my fingers closed on a half-full book of matches. I'd been wearing these jeans when Don and I had barbecued Saturday night, and I'd put the matches in my pocket rather than leave them outside where the incoming fog might ruin them. Pulling them out, I lit one and held it aloft.

It was a storeroom, all right, with makeshift shelves on three walls and the door in the fourth. What I had touched earlier was canned goods—tuna, vegetables, juice. Next to them were boxes of cereal, powdered milk, and sugar. The cloth was—

The match burned my fingers, and I dropped it. It went out when it hit the stone floor.

I lit another and checked the rest of the shelves. Stacks of olive drab fatigues such as Adair and Marchetti had been wearing. Rough gray blankets. Thin, hard-looking pillows. A mop and the bucket Adair had mentioned. Light bulbs and motor oil and a box labeled CANDLES.

The match went out. I lit another and reached into the box. The candles were small—plain tallow in glass cups, the kind you'd keep around in case there was a power failure. I set one on the shelf and lit it.

Now I could see a refrigerator against the wall opposite the door. Next to it were stacked cases of beer, the generic kind sold by chain supermarkets that just said BEER on the label. There were also cartons stacked on top of the 'fridge. I picked up the candle and raised it higher, looking for an escape route.

The shelves were around eight feet high and almost touched the ceiling. My eyes picked out a box of chocolate bars, and I went over and helped myself to one. Besides having an inordinate fondness for chocolate, I knew it was a quick energy source. And if I were to get out of here alive, I would need energy. I would also need warmth. My fingers, in spite of the heat from the matches and candle, were nearly frozen.

I went over to the stack of fatigues, rummaged through them, and selected a large pair. After pulling it on over my jeans and sweater, I had to roll up both the arms and legs, but it provided an extra layer of insulation from the cold. And if I got out of here, it would also make me less easy to spot in the dark.

The small candle was sputtering. I got another from the box and lit it with my second-to-last match. Then I held it high and began circling the room, looking for a way out—a heating duct, anything. When I moved the candle close to the boxes stacked on top of the refrigerator, I caught the glint of glass.

My pulse quickening, I set the light down and lifted a couple of boxes off the refrigerator. Behind them was a small window, about a yard long and two feet high, set close to the ceiling. It was grimy and I couldn't tell what it opened onto, but it was my escape route.

With sharpening determination, I moved the other boxes and stacked them in front of the refrigerator so I could climb on them. Then I looked around for something heavy.

There was a tool kit on one of the shelves, and in it I found a hammer. I looked at it and then at the window, thinking of the sound breaking glass would make. Could I smash the little window and be through it and away before anyone came to investigate? There was sure to be a drop on the other side, at least six feet, maybe more. What if I fell or turned an ankle? Then they would catch me, and I'd never be able to fool them with my helpless woman act again.

So what else can you do? I asked myself. Sit here in the dark, wondering what they plan for you?

I climbed up the boxes, crawled on top of the refrigerator, and took a close look at the window. The glass was thick, and I'd have to knock out most of the pane in order to slip through the small space without getting cut up. I paused, then raised the hammer and smashed it against the glass. It shattered, and some shards fell away outside, but not enough. The noise was deafening.

Desperately I whacked against the shards that still clung to the frame—one, two, three times. Most fell, but one jagged section refused to budge. I decided my heavy clothing would protect me, dropped the hammer, and began squeezing through the frame, feet first.

The casement slanted inward, and I almost slid down behind the refrigerator. Then I got my right leg hooked over the outside edge. I couldn't see the ground, and for a moment I panicked. What would I be jumping onto? What if—

There was a pounding of feet outside the door behind me. Hands fumbled at the padlock.

I took a deep breath and pushed off the sill with both hands. I was falling . . . and then I landed on hard ground. My left ankle gave a sharp pain, and I went down on my rear.

There were shouts from the room behind me. I scrambled to my feet. Ahead of me was what looked like a thickly planted stand of fir trees.

I ran.

chapter twenty-two

I ran across what seemed to be a graveled road and into the trees. Their low-hanging branches scratched my face and hands as I plunged through them. Needles and twigs snapped under my feet, and I could smell the bitter scent of pine sap. The shouts behind me grew fainter.

The ground was rocky and sloped down. At the bottom of the incline I heard the rush of water. The stream was not as big as the one near Levin's cabin, and I leaped over it and kept going—until I came to a stone wall maybe three yards beyond it.

I leaned against the wall, panting, then ran my hand over it. It was rough, but there were no crevices between the stones that could serve as handholds. Glancing up at its top, I thought I could make out a few strands of barbed wire. They might be part of an alarm system.

Did the wall surround the entire property? The only way to find out was to follow it and look for a break.

As I began moving along it to my right, I became aware of the sound of engines starting. Then there was a roar at the top of the slope, where the road was. Headlights washed over the thicket in front of the wall, and I dropped to the ground.

Around twenty feet away from me was what looked like the main gate to the property. Two jeeps, each containing a man, pulled up and waited. A guard holding a rifle came out of a shack next to the wall—a shack that looked incongruously like an outhouse. He opened the massive iron gates, waved the jeeps through, then returned to his post.

They were probably afraid I'd gotten over the wall already. The jeeps had been sent out to patrol the access roads for me.

I decided I had better find out how many of them I was up against, so I waited for a moment and then began to scale the incline on all fours. At the top, near the road, I lay on my stomach and peered through the underbrush.

The building I had escaped from, presumably the main building of the old winery, was a massive brick-and-stone structure set on a knoll. It had a peaked slate roof and ornamental towers at the corners; in each tower was mounted a floodlight and together they made the scene below as bright as day.

A semicircular driveway bisected the lawn in front of the building, and near the massive front doors stood four men in fatigues. Two of them carried rifles, but the others didn't appear to be armed. I didn't see Adair or Marchetti; probably they were somewhere inside. That made a minimum of nine men—two outside looking for me, the guard, four on the lawn, Marchetti and Adair inside. How many of them were armed? No matter how short their weapons supply, I was sure I could count on at least nine armed men.

And me, here in the dark, with no real sense of my bearings.

I moved quietly down the slope to the wall and started off along it in the opposite direction. Maybe it didn't go all the way around the property. Maybe there *was* a break.

After about fifty yards, the wall stopped, but instead of the break I'd been hoping for, I found a chain-link fence. It was as high as the wall and topped by three strands of barbed wire. It wouldn't have been difficult to climb, but I was certain it was wired with an alarm. I debated taking a chance, but decided against it. There had to be another way out besides the main gate; a military encampment would always have a secondary escape route. I kept going until the cover of trees became narrower and finally gave out.

Looking around, I pinpointed my location by the main building. I was behind it now, near the outbuildings I'd spotted from the hilltop the day before. The ruins of Levin's cabin would be to my left, beyond the fence and up a steep hill. Ahead I saw an open shed. It was lit; inside stood a jeep. Logically, their alternate escape route, if they had one, would be near where they had parked the jeeps.

I stood under cover of a pine tree, listening. It was quiet back here, although I could hear men shouting up toward the front gate.

They must still be searching for me up there. I took a chance and sprinted across the graveled road toward the shed.

Slipping along the wall, I looked inside, saw it was empty, and darted toward the jeep. There was a wrench sitting on a workbench; I picked it up and hurled it at the overhead bulb. In one lucky toss, the bulb shattered and all went black.

I moved along the driver's side of the jeep, hoping the keys were in the ignition. If they were, and if I found the escape route, I could steal the jeep and crash through the gate.

I stood up and reached for the ignition. A hand grabbed mine. I gasped with sudden terror.

"Relax, I already tried it," a familiar voice said softly. "No soap."

Willie.

I let out my breath in a relieved gust. My legs were trembling so hard I had to sit down in the driver's seat. Willie was hunched on the floor on the passenger side. All I could see was the glint of his eyes.

"Good Lord," I whispered when I could speak. "You almost scared the life out of me."

"You did a pretty good job on me too."

"What are you doing here?"

"Looking for you."

"How did you know they'd grabbed me—plus where they'd brought me?"

"Tell you later—there's no time now."

"You're right. We've got to get out of here. How'd you get in?"

"The back way, from Levin's cabin. The directions to it were all I had."

"The back way?" I turned to face him. "Then we can get out!"

"Nope. They must have forgot to close the gate; it was open when I got here. I scouted around, looking for you, then decided to go into Boulder Creek and get the law. When I went back, the gate was closed. There's an alarm."

"What kind of alarm?"

"Works on a weight principle. Obviously you can't have one that any field mouse or whatever they've got here could trip. But as soon as a person tries to climb that fence, all hell breaks loose."

"Bells?"

"Probably. Maybe lights too."

"Dammit."

I sat silently, listening for the sound of the search party. With what appeared to be limited personnel, they were probably still concentrating on the area where I'd gone out the window.

Willie reached out, plucked at the arm of the fatigues I'd put on, and said, "Nice threads. I could move a lot of these at the flea market. That's probably where the assholes picked them up."

"Yes." But what he'd just said had given me an idea. "How big a weight would it take to set off that alarm?"

"Couple of pounds. Why?"

"Do you know how it works?"

"I've seen them before. There's a wire. You get enough pressure to move it, it forces a connection, and bingo."

"Then I think I know what we can do." I reached down and unrolled one leg of the fatigues, then began pulling the hem out, making sure the pieces of thread were long ones.

"What the hell are you doing?"

"Hold these." When I had torn enough threads loose, I rolled the leg back up and got out of the jeep. "Come on. I assume you know how to trip this alarm."

"Sure, but that's the last thing we want."

"No, it's not." I led him out of the shed, slipped down its side, and started for the fence. "Show me where the best place to go over is."

"You mean to get to the road to Levin's cabin?"

"Yes."

He took the lead and we went around the long buildings, which he said were barracks, to a place where the fence was sheltered by eucalyptus. "We could go over here, and up the hill behind. It's a tough climb, but—"

Suddenly voices came from behind us. Willie grabbed me and we flattened in the tall weeds. The voices came on, and a light swept over where we were hidden. Footsteps crunched on gravel, and then became fainter.

It was minutes before we raised our heads. "Real assholes," Willie whispered. "They're out looking for you but they can't keep their fucking mouths shut."

"I think they're convinced I got over the wall. They sent two jeeps out. Probably the search party is just for form's sake."

"They're still assholes."

"Right." I stood up. "And that makes our job easier. Do you still have those threads I gave you?"

"Yes, ma'am."

"What we're going to do is trip the alarm by tying it with the threads. Then we hide. They come running, don't find anybody, and most likely won't see the threads either. The alarm will keep sounding, and eventually they'll cut it off. Then we go over the fence."

"I like it."

"Then let's go."

"Wait a minute," he said. "Where are we going to hide?"

"Lord, yes, we'd *better* decide that now."

"They'll be all over out here, beating the bush."

"And they'll know we're here this time, so they'll be more thorough."

Willie grinned suddenly, his teeth gleaming white in the moonlight. "Then why don't we hide where they'll least expect us?"

"Where?"

"Inside, in the barracks, under their own beds."

"I like *that*."

We slipped back to the barracks and reconnoitered. The one closest to the fence contained eight cots, most of them sloppily made up.

"What'd I tell you?" Willie whispered. "Assholes. You try that in the Corps, and you'd be busted to buck private." He went over to one cot and pulled the blankets nearly to the floor so they hid the space beneath it. I followed his lead and did the same to the one next to it. Then we tiptoed outside and went back to the fence.

It took all the threads we had, tied together in an elaborate spider-web arrangement that was strong but barely visible in the shadows. When it was constructed, Willie attached a final strand, waved me back toward the barracks, and pulled it taut. A siren went off in a moaning wail, and lights flashed on top of the fence. We turned and ran.

At the barracks, I dived under one of the cots, curling myself into a little ball and tugging to make sure the blankets touched the floor. Please, I thought, please don't let them come in here. And if they do, don't let them realize anything's different. Please let them be sloppy bed-makers from way back. . . .

As I always did at such moments, I wondered if I had reverted to praying. And if I had, what that meant—

There were shouts and running footsteps. It seemed like dozens of men were converging on the fence outside. The wailing of the siren continued. Somewhere close by a shot was fired. I flinched.

Minutes passed. Feet pounded past the barracks. Men called orders. Others cursed. But no one came into our hiding place.

After about five minutes, someone apparently remembered to cut off the alarm. The sounds of men searching continued, but finally they also subsided.

A few moments after that, Willie let out a sigh. "I think we did it."

"Yes. If they reconnect the alarm, it'll just start howling again. They'll think there's something wrong with it, and turn it off for good."

"So let's get going."

We crossed to the place we'd chosen to go over the fence. All was still around us. Willie gave me a hand up, and soon I had climbed over the barbed wire and down the other side. He followed.

"This way," he said, starting up the rocky hillside.

I went after him, sometimes on my hands and knees, taking in great breaths of the cool night air. I felt I hadn't breathed the whole time I'd been inside the compound, and the oxygen hurt my lungs, still tender from the chloroform. We stopped and rested several times on our climb, looking back at the lights of the encampment below.

When we finally reached the meadow near the ruins of Levin's cabin, we both collapsed on the grass. I flopped over on my back, staring up at the black sky. The stars shone coldly and steadily, like shaved ice.

After a few moments, I said to Willie, "Tell me how you knew they'd brought me here."

"I called in and got your message at the Oasis. You said you would be late, but that you'd meet me. I knew I hadn't set anything up. Then I found your car in the parking lot behind the Villa Romana. And this in the alley behind the Oasis."

I sat up and looked at what he held. It was one of my earrings. I put my hand to my earlobe. Funny, I hadn't even noticed the earring was gone.

Willie handed it to me and I put it back on. I said, "How did you know it was mine?"

"You had it on Saturday at the flea market."

"Most men wouldn't remember a thing like that."

"You forget—Alida was a jewelry designer." There was an empty note in his voice. I reached out and squeezed his arm.

"But how did you know to come here?" I asked.

"By then I'd put enough of it together to know who would want to grab you. I'd suspected Mack and Monty and that Jerry Levin were up to something for a long time. When Levin started watching me, I got real nervous. So I pretended I didn't know who he was and hired you to find out what was going on."

"Why didn't you just tell me the whole story?"

"I suspected they were up to something big, and I didn't want to mess with them at all if I could help it. Stupid of me, I guess. Anyway, by this afternoon, I knew what they were doing, but not where. Then I talked to that rabbi and the other guy about Levin's cabin. You'd told me about somebody shooting at you down here. It was enough."

"You're not such a bad detective after all."

"Thanks."

"Willie," I said, figuring I stood as good a chance of getting it out of him now as ever, "where were you when Jerry Levin was shot?"

"That's kind of private."

"Don't you think I deserve to know?"

"Yeah." He sighed. "I guess you do. I was with Sam's lady, Carolyn Bui."

"What?"

"It's not what you think. Carolyn's a friend; so's Sam. I was trying to help them."

"How?"

"Well, as you probably can tell, Sam's not easy to live with. Carolyn loves him, but lately that love has gotten worn out. She started running around on Sam, with lots of different guys, and one of them turned out to be a decent human being. Carolyn fell in love, and she wants to leave Sam, but she's afraid what it will do to him."

"Where do you come into this?"

"I've been meeting her on Sunday nights while Sam's packing up at the flea market, just for a couple of hours, so she would have somebody who understands to talk it out with. That's why I didn't tell the cops where I was."

"Surely Carolyn wouldn't have minded—"

"Of course not. But don't you see—it was their private business, not something to be stuck in a police report."

"Did Sam know you were talking with Carolyn?"

"He suspected, but he had it all wrong. Monty—that little snake—saw us together at the Oasis a couple of times. He said something to Sam. Sam accused Carolyn of having an affair with me, but she managed to talk him out of that idea."

So that was how Adair had known Willie wouldn't be home at five o'clock on Sunday afternoon, and had had Selena tell Levin that. "You're a hell of a good friend, Willie," I said.

"Nah, I just don't have many friends, is all. I do right by the few I've got." We sat there in silence for a minute, and then Willie said, "Let's get going."

We crossed the meadow, skirted the ruins of the cabin, and went over the little bridge to the road where Sam's old van stood. Willie reached in his pocket, handed me a set of keys, and said, "Here, you go into Boulder Creek and get the law."

"And where will you be?"

"I'm going back."

"What?"

"I've got a score to settle." He patted his denim jacket down around the beltline, and I realized he had a gun concealed there. He'd had it all along. "I'm going to take out Marchetti and Adair and as many of the others as I can."

He turned and started down the driveway to the bridge.

"Willie, if that's the gun you took off Selena, it's hardly a weapon at all," I said. "If it were such a terrific gun, you'd have used it while we were in there."

"Don't worry about me." He kept going.

"Willie." I followed him. "Willie, this isn't you. You don't believe in killing."

"Now I do." He started up the slope to the cabin.

I walked faster. "They'll kill *you*."

"Not before I get some of them."

"Listen, this is stupid."

"A man does what he has to do."

"Now you sound like one of them. You sound like a redneck right-wing asshole!"

He kept going, into the redwoods by the cabin.

"Willie, neither Adair nor Marchetti killed Jerry Levin." I hadn't known it long, but I believed it now.

He turned, his face surprised in the dim light. "So who did?"

"I can't tell you yet."

"Well, it doesn't matter. Alida's the one I care about, and one of them killed her. I figured out enough to know that. She was coming to see me, and she saw one of them split with those Torahs and recognized him." He started walking again toward the hillside.

I wasn't going to let him do it. Whatever his faults, I cared about Willie. He had a big heart—too big, maybe—and a love of life. I wasn't going to let that life end.

I looked around for the biggest, heaviest stick I could find and hefted it. Then I went after him. I came up behind him and raised that stick and whacked him right on the head, as hard as I'd ever hit another human being.

He said, "Unh?" and went down on his knees. And then he pitched forward, flat on his face, out cold.

I stood looking down at him, feeling more than a twinge of remorse. A pity, I thought, a real pity.

Why couldn't it have been Leo McFate instead?

chapter twenty-three

I found Sam Thomas at dawn. He was sitting on the hard-packed earth above the beach near his house, drinking beer and staring off at the pier that was part of the sewer project. The sun was coloring the houses on the hills behind me, but the sea was still shrouded in fog; the end of the long pier disappeared into it.

When my footsteps crunched on the gravel of the parking lot, Sam turned his head slightly, then looked back to sea.

My fingers closed over the butt of the gun I had in my bag, the gun I'd picked up at home, tiptoeing so I wouldn't wake Don and alarm him. I sensed I wouldn't need to use it, however. Sam's slumped shoulders were those of a man who had lost, and knew it. Perhaps he'd known it for a long time.

"What took you so long?" He spoke plaintively, as if I'd broken a promise.

I came up behind him. "Were you expecting me?"

"You, the cops, someone." He drained his beer can and hurled it down toward the beach. It clattered against the dirt slope and fell soundlessly to the sand. There was a paper bag that looked like it contained a six-pack next to him. He pulled out another beer and popped the tab.

I sat down next to him, my hand still on the gun. I was bone-tired and sad, and I wanted to get this over with. But it wouldn't come to an end for many hours; I hadn't yet begun to deal with the police.

After I'd knocked Willie out, I'd dragged him to Sam's van—not without considerable difficulty—and headed for Boulder Creek. He came to on the drive and by the time we found a phone booth at a gas station, he'd started to listen to reason. I called Hank and told him what had happened and said that I was bringing Willie and one of the killers in. I told him Marchetti and Adair and the other members of their group were probably still at the encampment. Hank said he would alert both the San Francisco police and the Boulder Creek authorities. He also said I'd damned well better deliver Willie or we'd be in more trouble than he could handle. I promised I would. Then we headed north in the van.

I had stopped at home for the gun, and then Willie and I went to Sam's house. Carolyn, very pale and looking like she hadn't slept in days, told me where to find Sam. I left Willie with her and walked over to the beach.

Now Sam said, "Carolyn tell you where I was?"

"Yes."

"I said she should tell anyone who came. I'd not hiding anything; I'm not trying to avoid responsibility. I just came over here because I couldn't sleep." He paused. "You guessed all of it, didn't you?"

"Yes."

"How?"

"From a few things people said. And one you did."

"About Jerry Levin being bald under that skullcap."

"That's right. I should have noticed it at the time. You said you'd only seen him once, at David's with Selena. He wouldn't have taken the cap off there; you had to have seen his head the way I did."

"With his brains blown out and the cap on the floor next to him. Yeah."

"Carolyn caught it too. Did you tell her about killing him?"

"I had to. It was so pathetic, the way that little cap rolled off his head after he fell on the floor."

"And that's why you can't sleep."

"I haven't been able to sleep for years." He crumpled his beer can and stared at its mangled shape. "What else made you realize I'd done it?"

"Well, it would have been easy for you to get keys to Willie's house. And Willie told me you suspected he was having an affair with Carolyn. You knew he wouldn't be home that Sunday afternoon. I wouldn't have understood how you got hold of Monty Adair's gun if Adair hadn't told me he kept illegal things—hot merchandise and controlled substances, he called them—stashed in Willie's garage."

Sam looked surprised. "So that's whose it was. I went there looking for some kind of proof about Willie and Carolyn. I know now that she was telling the truth when she said there was nothing between them, but at the time I was sure I'd find something. I wanted to drag it out in front of her, shove it under her self-righteous nose. Instead, I found this nice little stash. But I couldn't figure out whose it was; I knew Willie never did drugs and wouldn't own a gun. Monty's, huh?"

"Yes."

"In a way it's kind of funny." But he didn't look amused.

"Sam," I said, "why Levin? Why did you have to kill him?"

"I didn't have to. It just happened."

"How?"

"He came in through that side door from the passageway. This was right after I found the stash. I heard him coming and hid. He started poking around in the garage, looking for something—those Torahs, I know now.

"I'd grabbed the stash bag and taken it with me when I hid. The gun was there in it. I pulled it out, sneaked up behind Levin. And then I . . . I blew him away."

"Why, Sam?"

"I don't know. It was like a flashback. I was trapped there, and all of a sudden it was like being back in 'Nam. I didn't even think about it. I just blew him away."

I shuddered, picturing the cold-blooded act.

Sam opened another beer. "I know what you're thinking—that it was horrible. But it wasn't, not really. I'd done so many worse things in 'Nam. And he was lying there, kind of peaceful. If it hadn't been for that hat falling off, and his pathetic little bald spot . . ."

"What did you do then?"

"Wiped the gun off so my fingerprints wouldn't be on it. Messed the house up so it would look like a robbery."

"Why?"

"I don't know. I wasn't thinking so clear. I guess it occurred to me that if the police thought he was a burglar they wouldn't look so hard for whoever killed him. Then I got out of there, but I couldn't go far; I wanted to see what would happen. And, man, things did."

"Like what?"

"First Mack Marchetti showed up, only about fifteen minutes later. He went in the same way Levin had, and came out fast. I could see his face was white, even from where I was parked across the street. It made me feel good; Marchetti's such a macho son-of-a-bitch; it's good to know he couldn't take it."

Unfortunately, it also meant he hadn't the presence of mind to search for the Torahs—the exact location of which Adair had neglected to tell him—and had had to come back the next night, when Alida spotted him. I didn't want to remind Sam of that, however. "Then what happened?"

"Marchetti took off. Willie arrived about six-thirty. He didn't go in, though, just stuck the sign on the door about being at the Oasis. A few minutes later Roger Beck came by, and right after him, Monty. They both saw the sign and split."

"And then?"

"Alida showed. That shook me. I figured she had keys to Willie's house, and I didn't want her going in there and finding Levin. I mean, Alida could be a pain in the ass sometimes, but she was really a very nice lady. She didn't deserve that kind of trouble."

"So you went up there and asked her to take your cash to Willie at the Oasis."

"Yeah. I watched to make sure she left and then I split too. I figured Willie would be the next person to go into the house, and I knew he could do whatever had to be done."

I sighed. There it all was. Senseless. As senseless and sad as the war that had crippled Sam Thomas's mind and made all of this possible.

He continued drinking beer and looking out to sea. The sun had cleared the hills by now, and I could feel its warmth touching my shoulders. Above us gulls wheeled in the sky, looking for breakfast.

"Sam," I finally said, "why don't you come with me and we'll talk to the police."

"Not yet. Just let me stay here a little bit more. They're going to put me away for a long time."

"Maybe someone can help you."

"Nobody can. Carolyn couldn't."

No, I thought, she couldn't. But did she really try?

We sat there, watching the fog lift and the sun highlight the water. Finally Sam finished his last beer and stood up. He took a final look at the sea, and then we walked back to his house together.

chapter twenty-four

I lifted the lid of the pot, let the steam clear, and then sniffed its contents. Something was not right here. "Oregano," I said, "maybe it needs more oregano."

"I'd be careful; that's powerful stuff." Willie sat at my kitchen table, drinking beer and—by all intents—supervising.

"Garlic, then?"

He just looked at me.

"Well, I don't know. I wanted to make a nice dinner for Don when he comes back and announces he's got the job at the radio station. But I can't make this sauce smell right!"

"Sit down and have some wine." Willie reached for a bottle of Chianti and poured some in a glass.

I put the lid back on the pot and flopped down at the table.

"How come you can't cook?" Willie asked.

I glared at him and picked up my wine. "I can. I bake terrifi bread."

"So?"

"This is different. With bread it's like playing with a chemistry set—everything is timed, and the temperature has to be just so."

"That sounds harder than marinara sauce."

"Not really. You just follow directions, plus you get to play with the dough, kneading it." I stared glumly at the pot on the stove, then checked my watch. Don had said he would be back by five, and it was quarter of now.

Willie went to the racing-striped refrigerator and got another beer. "You were going to tell me the latest word on Marchetti and Adair."

"Oh, right. I got so carried away by my culinary efforts that I forgot. They caught Marchetti down near Santa Barbara; probably he was heading for Mexico. He's not talking, but they canvassed the area around your house and came up with a couple of witnesses who can place him there at the time of Alida's murder. One even saw her following him, so I think they can build a pretty strong case. The police agree with my theory that she saw him leave your house, followed to see what he'd taken, and he killed her to keep her from reporting it."

Willie's face darkened and he took a swig of beer, but he didn't say anything. Characteristically, he was keeping a tight rein on his emotions regarding Alida's death.

"Anyway," I went on, "the police have also tied Marchetti to the theft of the Torahs and the Levin business because he had two sets of keys to your house on him—the one he used, and the other that he took off Levin's body."

"Why'd he bother to do that?"

"Didn't want any link at all; in case Selena talked, there wouldn't be any proof Levin had ever had the keys."

"That's another thing I don't understand—if Levin knew he was going to get those keys, why did he put on that act for you and make the appointment to meet us?"

I shrugged. "Insurance, probably. If for some reason he couldn't find the Torahs at your place, he could then try to talk you into hunting for them and turning them over to him."

"Do you think he was sincere about this religious conversion?"

"I don't think we'll ever know. Selena thought so, but she's a romantic and also pretty gullible. But on the other hand, Monty Adair believed it, and he's as cynical and hard-headed as they come."

"Speaking of Monty, what about him?"

"For starters, the police have him on kidnapping. Plus, there's his complicity in the thefts."

"Good. I'd like to see the little weasel put away for a long time."

"He will be."

"A lot of good that'll do me, though. I've lost two runners, and after this mess, the cops'll be watching every move I make."

"At least you're not in jail for murder."

"There's that." He was silent for a moment, and then his face brightened. "Actually, I been thinking. Maybe it's about time I went legit."

"Oh?"

"Yeah. I'm a damn sharp trader, and if I didn't have to mess with phony receipts and deposits—not to mention the kind of scuzzballs I've got to deal with—well, there's no telling what kind of bucks I might make."

I was pleased, but I said only, "You should think it over."

"I am. Yes, ma'am, that might be just the way to go. It'd be sure to put the cops' noses out of joint if they were never able to get anything on me."

I grinned. "It certainly would."

Finishing my wine, I got up and went back to the stove. The mixture in the pot smelled the same. I was stirring it, hoping a little agitation would produce an improvement, when I heard the front door open. Don called out and came down the hall. He was carrying a bottle of champagne and a conical package from a florist's shop.

"You got the job!" I dropped the spoon in the pot and hurried over to him.

"Yes—and it's even better than I thought. Here." He thrust the flowers at me. They were red-and-white carnations with one perfect rose in the center.

I set the flowers carefully on the table and hugged him. "I'm so glad. Really I am."

He kissed me lightly, then studied my face. "You mean that, don't you?"

"Yes. We'll have that talk soon, and then you'll understand." It was the truth: the last few days had reminded me that there are far worse things to fear in this world than the failure of love. I'd just have to learn to cope with emotional fear the way I did with the physical variety.

He kissed me again and said, "Let's break out the champagne."

Willie stood up. "I think I better be going."

Don waved him back into his chair. "Stay. You've got reason to celebrate, too."

He popped the champagne cork while I got glasses. The wine

bubbled over, but he got it poured in time. We toasted—to Willie, to me, to Don's new job.

"So tell us about it," I said.

He smiled broadly, tipping back his chair. "I'm not going to be just any d.j."

"Oh no?"

"No indeed. You are looking at the host of KSUN's new celebrity talk show."

"You're kidding!"

"I'm not. They liked my demo tape, but the thing they liked most was the way I handled the teenage callers."

"Amazing." The call-ins were the part of the show Don hated most. There was no way he could do them wearing earplugs.

"Well, they did, so they proposed a talk show. I get a celebrity on there—someone who's performing in town and looking for publicity—and ask him questions. We'll take call-ins too, but they'll be carefully screened."

"Is it good money?" Willie asked.

"The best. Of course, I'll still have to do a rock-and-roll show, but several times a week I'll get to do the other. And they said to make it as controversial as I like." His eyes gleamed, and I knew he was thinking of how to create radio's most embarrassing moments. For a man who hated rock-and-roll as much as Don, the job had fascinating possibilities.

"Well, here's to fortune and fame." Willie raised his glass. "When do you move?"

"As soon as I can find a place large enough for my baby grand piano." Don glanced at me and winked.

I gave an inward sigh of relief, not returning the wink because I never winked at anyone. The last hurdle had been crossed; he didn't intend to move in with me. He understood my need to go slowly and carefully.

"So what's for dinner?" Don stood up and went to the stove.

"Um, it was going to be lasagna," I said, "but I'm not too sure about the marinara sauce."

Don raised the pot lid.

"I'd take it kind of easy," Willie said.

I glared at him.

Don sniffed at the sauce, drew back, and then sniffed again. "Come here," he said to Willie.

Willie went over there and Don pointed at the sauce, indicating he should smell it. Willie looked hesitant. Don said, "I insist."

Willie sniffed gingerly. Then he straightened up and looked at Don.

"What do you think?" Don asked.

Willie shrugged.

"No, really."

"I think we should continue this celebration over dinner."

"Right." Don turned to me. "Babe, would you do us the honor of accompanying us to dinner tonight? There's a wonderful little Italian restaurant that just opened over on Union Street. . . ."